PERMANENT SUNSET

PERMANENT SUNSET

A Sabrina Salter Mystery

C. Michele Dorsey

CROOKED
LANE

NEW YORK

Published in the United States by Crooked Lane Books, an imprint of The Quick Brown Fox & Company LLC.

Crooked Lane Books and its logo are trademarks of The Quick Brown Fox & Company LLC.

Library of Congress Catalog-in-Publication data available upon request.

ISBN (hardcover): 978-1-62953-770-2
ISBN (ePub): 978-1-62953-795-5
ISBN (Kindle): 978-1-62953-796-2
ISBN (ePDF): 978-1-62953-797-9

Cover and book design by Jennifer Canzone.

Printed in the United States.

www.crookedlanebooks.com

Crooked Lane Books
34 West 27th St., 10th Floor
New York, NY 10001

First Edition: October 2016

10 9 8 7 6 5 4 3 2 1

For John Holmes and Victor Posada
Love is kind.

Chapter One

"Do you think she signed the prenup?" Henry asked Sabrina as she drove them through the early morning light toward Villa Nirvana on Ditleff Point in Fish Bay. A short morning rain shower, typical on the island of St. John in the Virgin Islands, had just finished. Sabrina hoped there would be no more precipitation that day, but on an island, you could never be sure. It could be pouring in Coral Bay, yet sunny and clear in Cruz Bay eight miles away. She hoped for one of St. John's spectacular sunsets for the wedding at the villa, since the bride had insisted the ceremony be conducted precisely as the sun went down. But even in paradise, a sunset could occasionally fizzle.

"I don't know. Do you think he'll go through with the wedding if she doesn't sign?" In less than twelve hours, about fifty of the island's "rich and famous" were scheduled to attend the wedding of Sean Michael Keating and Elena Consuela Soto Rodriguez at Villa Nirvana—that is, if Elena decided to sign a prenuptial agreement. Sean had apparently presented it to her weeks before. So far, she had not executed it.

Sabrina still wondered why she ever let Henry talk her into submitting a proposal to manage Villa Nirvana, St. John's newest luxury villa. It made their business, Ten Villas, top-heavy with an eleventh. They had their first real fight as business partners over the decision.

"Nirvana is in such a different league than our other ten villas; I don't see it as a good fit. I'm in favor of keeping it simple and uncomplicated." Of course she was. Both Sabrina and Henry had fled Massachusetts a few years earlier, each escaping their own versions of unhappy endings. She had fled to St. John after being acquitted of murdering her husband on Nantucket. Henry's career at an airline had tanked in public disgrace, sending him off to the island with Sabrina, his good friend. They had eased into a life of obscurity and simple contentment that had almost been destroyed a few months earlier when a guest had been murdered at one of their villas. The last thing Sabrina wanted now was to risk more attention and trouble. The kind of people who could afford to stay at Villa Nirvana seemed to be magnets for drama and notoriety.

But Henry's arguments had prevailed. "We don't have to live there, Sabrina. We only have to manage it. We will make oodles of money and prove ourselves as one of the top villa management companies on the island." Since Sabrina's objections came from her gut, hardly a rational basis for a business decision, she had yielded to Henry's logic.

The wedding was Villa Nirvana's inaugural event, meticulously planned by the couple and other family members. Their fledgling company owned Villa Nirvana, the first luxury villa built by Keating Construction. Sean and Elena had been clear with Henry and Sabrina that the wedding needed to be perfect because the attendees were targeted clients. Sabrina knew that if the wedding got called off, there would be more than one business casualty.

After the rehearsal dinner last evening, when most of the other guests had gone, Sabrina and Henry and their very curious staff couldn't help but overhear the family arguing in the vast and open great room.

"You're a Harvard Business grad, for God's sake. You know a prenup makes sense," the groom's brother, Gavin, had told Elena.

"It doesn't make sense to me," Elena said, erupting into a wail.

"It protects you, too," her future father-in-law said.

"It protects the company but undermines the future of my marriage to your son, whom I adore," Elena said, her howling escalating.

"Dear, all the Keating wives have signed prenups and have gone on to have enduring marriages," Elena's future mother-in-law said, trying to comfort and persuade her.

"Well, I am not yet a Keating wife and choose not to be one if this is how the family regards its women."

Sabrina had noticed the only person not trying to convince Elena was her future husband.

Elena eventually tore out of the great room and retreated into the master bedroom, temporarily dubbed the bridal suite and reserved for her exclusive use. Various family members had continued to approach her as envoys, pleading with her to be "reasonable" and appreciate that it was "only business."

When Henry and Sabrina had finally closed the kitchen after preparing for the extended brunch that would be served the next morning, Elena was still screaming.

"I will not be treated this way just because I come from a poor Puerto Rican family. You either love me and want me to be your wife or you don't." They had heard a door slam, but Sabrina knew that may not have been the end of the debate.

The following morning, Sabrina got out of the passenger seat to open the stately wrought-iron gate that secluded Ditleff Point from the rest of St. John. She recalled when Elena had given her and Henry the code to the keypad, along with a strict admonishment not to give it to anyone else, not even their "underlings."

Villa Nirvana was built on the farthest point of a low-lying outcrop off Fish Bay. The outcrop rose at the end and was surrounded by cliffs upon which waves crashed relentlessly. Until last year when construction had started, Ditleff Point was just a long, undeveloped elbow of raw land extending from the coast, where people hiked and deer frolicked. Sabrina had hiked it several times while on vacation before moving to St. John. She wished it hadn't been developed.

Now Villa Nirvana was a sprawling 12,000-square-foot home built of native stone with an additional 5,000 square feet of outdoor living space. It had enough room to sleep twenty.

It was the first of six island homes to be built on Ditleff Point. Nirvana had a state-of-the-art kitchen, a bar, and a great room with an infinity pool outside. On the lower level, there was an underground media room, a separate commercial-grade kitchen, and a wine cellar. With solar panels and a helicopter pad, the home was so excessively luxurious, Sabrina felt repelled by it. Nirvana just didn't mesh with Sabrina's vision of the business she and Henry had grown from scratch. And if she was honest, she had to admit the villa reminded her just a tad of the massive stone waterfront home in Massachusetts where her mother had grown up and where her grandmother still lived—a home Sabrina had never entered.

They parked in a spot next to the service entrance to the kitchen, passing the beach/pool cabana, and entered the quiet house without speaking. Once in the kitchen, Sabrina spotted a figure sitting at the large stainless steel counter, hunched over a mug.

"Sean?" Sabrina spoke softly, not wanting to startle the normally animated young businessman. Before hiring Ten Villas, he and Elena had put Henry and Sabrina through an interview process as thorough as if they were applying for a position at the White House.

The young man, still on the sunny side of forty, looked up at her with red-rimmed eyes, dark circles accentuating the grimness of his expression. His thick, dark hair fell on his forehead. Sabrina imagined he'd run his hands through it a thousand times during the night.

"Am I in your way here?" He started to rise from the sleek metal stool he was sitting on.

"No, we're just here to set up coffee and beverages until the Triple B's breakfast truck arrives," Sabrina said, watching as Henry softly pushed the button to the commercial coffee maker they had set up the night before.

Sabrina appreciated that Sean had made some savvy choices for the weekend wedding celebration. He had seized the opportunity to ingratiate himself and his new luxury villa construction business with the existing St. John business community. He had chosen a funky gourmet breakfast truck to serve brunch from 8:00 until 1:00. Guests would then be taken on tours of the island in safari trucks driven by locals. The rehearsal dinner had been delectable Mediterranean tapas from the Little Olive food truck, served with fine wines from the Nirvana wine cellar. The juxtaposition of truck food with an opulent setting made a statement. Sean understood the two sides to St. John. Zeus, the premier restaurant on island, would cater the wedding dinner.

"Can I pour you a glass of fresh orange juice?" Henry asked, reaching into the Sub-Zero refrigerator. He and

Sabrina had squeezed a dozen containers of juices the night before while being entertained by the Keating clan screaming at each other. They had to be very careful not to smudge the thick vanilla frosting on the wedding cake when putting items in the refrigerator. It had so many flowers on it, it wouldn't fit in a box. Just another thing to worry about, Sabrina had complained.

"No, I'll get out of your way and wait for the coffee," Sean said. Sabrina noticed he was wearing the same clothes as the night before.

"So, am I officiating at my first wedding today or not?" Henry asked.

Sabrina suppressed a gasp at his boldness. Sometimes Henry was more direct than she thought wise. She knew he was nervous. The Ministry of Matrimony had recently issued each of them impressive looking certificates, which proclaimed Henry and Sabrina were officially authorized to join two people in marriage, another part of Henry's business plan. Sabrina hated the idea and hoped never to have to use it. But Henry was thrilled about performing weddings and had volunteered to officiate at Sean and Elena's, which worked for Sean personally as it fit his own business plan: get the locals on your side.

"Yes, you will, Henry. Although I'm not sure whether my family will be attending. I need to go to Elena and let her know I don't need a prenup, and if my family does, well, screw them. She was so upset last night. I've never seen her hysterical like that. She has to be exhausted. I've been waiting for her to wake up to tell her I don't care about a prenup."

Henry slapped Sean on the back, again horrifying Sabrina.

"Good for you, Sean. You're the one getting married to Elena, not your family. She might like it if you wake her up with the news. I'm sure she'll be just as relieved as you are."

Sabrina cringed. She wondered again if Henry was stepping over the line. Henry's experience working for years as a first-class flight attendant seemed to help him gauge what were acceptable boundaries for people. Sabrina had no such frame of reference. She was always looking out for what was considered proper. After Sabrina's mother had bolted when she was a toddler, she was left to learn social grace from her alcoholic father and a diner owner who became her mother figure. If it hadn't been for self-help books, she wasn't sure what she would have done.

But Sean didn't seem offended and set off to find his bride, who Sabrina couldn't help but note was not sharing the bridal suite quite yet with her husband-to-be. Sean had been given a room of his own. This state of affairs seemed very old-fashioned and not consistent with Sabrina's image of Elena. The few times she had met the bride, Elena had been dressed in an Armani suit, wearing heels so high they reminded Sabrina of the shoes she had been forced to wear when she was a television meteorologist in Boston. Elena had that "well-put-together" look that Sabrina didn't trust after years of working with people so coated with veneer that she couldn't recognize them without their perfect outfits and layers of makeup. Seeing Elena unraveled and behaving like a banshee the night before had made Sabrina curious about how many layers were hidden beneath her glossy surface.

She helped Henry load a cart with freshly squeezed orange and grapefruit juices along with coffee, and Henry wheeled it out into a corner of the great room where guests could help themselves when they got up. Midmorning, buckets filled with ice and bottles of Prosecco and champagne would be added to the offerings.

Sabrina thought she heard the sound of the Triple B's food truck arriving outside when Sean dashed back into the kitchen, wearing what could only be described as an anguished expression.

"She's gone. I can't find her. She must have left because of the prenup. I should have told my father and brother to drop it. I knew it."

"Are all her things gone?" Sabrina asked, thinking Elena might have decided to take an early morning walk or run—the petite bride-to-be didn't have an ounce of fat on her shapely body. And Sabrina doubted that Elena would be able to pack up and leave in the middle of the night with the extensive wardrobe she'd seen in the closet. There were a few rental vehicles, provided by Ten Villas for guests to use, parked by the service entrance. But where would she go? You needed to take a ferry or have access to a private boat to get off the island.

"Her clothes are there, but I didn't see her wedding dress. The big white plastic cover that was on it when she arrived is empty and sitting on the bed, which was still made," Sean said.

"Maybe she went to talk to someone from her family staying elsewhere on island. Are there people you can call?" Sabrina saw the panic in Sean's face. She couldn't blame him. No one wanted to be left at the altar, and this was damn close to it. And frankly, the last thing she and Henry needed was for their first huge event at Nirvana to turn into a fiasco.

"That's just it. She has no family. That's why she was so excited to become part of mine and was so hurt when they all wanted her to sign the prenup like she was some gold digger."

From outside, Sabrina heard the voices of Amy and Erin of the Triple B, which stood for "two babes on a bay." The Triple B normally served breakfast on weekends in Coral Bay on the other, more remote side of St. John.

Soon the villa's occupants would be rising, going for a run or a swim in the infinity pool. Wedding guests, who had been invited for a full day of celebration starting with breakfast, would begin arriving. It seemed important for life to look as normal as possible while they figured out where the missing bride was.

"Henry, could you please keep everything calm here while Sean and I do a casual search of the property? Elena may have just needed some time to herself after the drama last night."

"Of course. I'm sure you'll find that she's just taken a stroll on the beach," Henry said.

"You think she just might have wanted a little space from the pressure my family was putting on her?" Sean sounded desperate to believe that Elena was just off having a good pout or cry.

"When I peeked in on her just before we left last night, she had the wedding dress on and seemed pretty sad. She said she wasn't sure she'd get to wear it tomorrow, so she was going to enjoy it while she could. I can't imagine she went anywhere in that dress," Henry said, looking at Sabrina, who didn't try to hide her disapproving expression. She hadn't known Henry went to counsel the bride before they left Villa Nirvana the night before. Sometimes it seemed what she lacked in social confidence, Henry had in excess.

"We'd better get going. We've only got a few hours to find her and set this right," Sabrina said.

"If it can be," said Sean.

"Wait, you can't be seen in yesterday's clothes on your wedding day; everyone will know something is wrong." Henry sent him off to freshen up before the search for the missing bride began.

Chapter Two

Sabrina knew Henry was waiting for her to scold him. She said nothing.

"What, don't you want to tell me it was incredibly stupid to go and talk to Elena before we left last night? I knew you'd think so. That's why I didn't mention it before."

Sabrina looked up from the checklist for the brunch after ticking off three items.

"You already know it was dumb. You don't need me to tell you that, especially not with six of the waitstaff about to enter the kitchen door."

She couldn't help but enjoy this. He had been so adamant about getting the contract for Nirvana, never really listening to her objections. Why had he been so bullheaded? And now their first function, the wedding of the villa owner, a young entrepreneur who was considered one of the most eligible bachelors in the country, was about to tank.

Sabrina knew Henry wanted to show his former fellow employees that he had rebounded from Allied Air's grossly unfair treatment of him—they had fired him for sexual harassment rather than confront the married pilot who had been pursuing him. Henry Whitman had been humiliated by an airline that he had considered family. His own father had been an Allied pilot and his mother worked as a stewardess, as they were then called, until she had Henry.

Now he had climbed out from under the rubble of disgrace and had created a little gem of a business on his own, rubbing elbows with powerful business executives who would attract media attention. She wondered whether Henry wasn't secretly trying to show his ex-lover, David, how misguided he'd been not to choose Henry over a wife he didn't love. Maybe he saw Villa Nirvana as his redemption. Instead, he was going to be associated with one of the biggest social debacles of the year.

"Okay, I'm ready. What are we going to say to people?" Sean returned to the kitchen looking as if he'd just swallowed eight hours of sleep. His deep tan contrasted with a cream-colored silk shirt and khaki shorts. He wore a pair of Sperry boat shoes with just enough scuffs to show he really did own a boat. Sean was the picture of island living. With the help of a pair of Ray Bans, no one would know he'd had a sleepless night.

"You just leave that to me," Sabrina said, opening the door for the brunch truck crew.

Sabrina led Sean out of the kitchen into an open corridor with arched windows that looked out at the sea, giving the impression that if you jumped out of one of them, you'd cannonball into the Caribbean. The truth was there were jagged cliffs beneath the windows, so steep you could only see them if you approached the edge of the property and peered directly down.

They almost collided with Jack Keating, Sean's father and the CEO of Keating Construction, the leading parking garage construction firm in the country. Tall and lean, Jack was a wrinkled version of his handsome son, except that his hair was thick silver. Sabrina marveled at how some people just looked rich.

"There you are. Did Elena sign the damn prenup? She should know this isn't personal. I'm thrilled she's joining the family, and she's been a great asset to the business, but we can't be stupid about things now, can we?"

Sure we can, Sabrina thought, waiting to hear whether Sean would stand up to his father.

"No, she didn't sign, at least not that I know. And it's okay, Dad, because I'm going to marry her anyway. We're not going to get divorced, and even if we do years from now, you know Elena will bring in more money to the business than she could ever cost. Look what's she's already done, having us move the company headquarters to St. Thomas," Sean said.

"Well, yes, but then there's your brother and Lisa."

"Lisa chose to sign a prenup fifteen years ago, and she's never been associated with the business. Elena isn't going to be a housewife. You know that."

"Well, what about your mother? She signed one too, you know," Jack said, but Sabrina could hear his heart wasn't in the argument.

"Of course she did. She saw how much Gavin's mother skinned you for in the divorce. She knew how much you had sacrificed to marry her. Mom has never been about money. Isn't that part of what made you fall for her?"

"You should have gone to law school. You'd have made a helluva courtroom lawyer."

"What, and not be here to shift the company from building parking garages to luxury residences in the Caribbean? Dad, you are going to love seeing the company grow with the plans Elena and I have. You may even change your mind about retiring in three years."

Sabrina shifted forward a small step to remind the Keating men she was there.

"Sir, did you happen to see Elena this morning? They've moved up her hair appointment and we need to let her know." She was pleased by how smoothly she fibbed. Henry would be proud.

Jack looked at Sabrina as if he just noticed her.

"Nope. The only person I've seen was the backside of my wife slipping out the door of our room at dawn with her easel. Off to capture the Caribbean at dawn *en plein air*, she said."

"Okay, well the Triple B brunch truck will be serving brunch shortly. There are lots of Ten Villa servers here to help you if you don't want to go out to the truck to place your order," Sabrina said, wanting to move on and search for Elena.

"Truck food? I love it. I'm an old construction worker. Great idea. For once, I think I am really going to enjoy a wedding."

Sabrina suggested that they check with Sean's half brother, Gavin, next. She knocked on the door, stepping aside so Sean would take the stage. Gavin opened the door with a jerk.

"I hope you're here to tell me you've got that woman under control and she signed the goddamn prenup," Gavin Keating said.

Sabrina noticed Gavin was already up, dressed in slacks and a golf shirt, and had CNN on the forty-eight-inch flat-screen television that each of the bedrooms was equipped with.

"We're just here to remind you that Triple B will begin serving brunch at eight, but there are beverages available in the great room right now," Sabrina said.

Gavin looked at Sabrina and ignored her. Sabrina felt her jaw tighten as Gavin silently dismissed her. She'd had plenty of men at the television station where she had been a meteorologist treat her as if she were invisible. Sexism in the television industry had been rampant, but Gavin

Keating's condescending attitude went beyond that. Sabrina smelled a misogynist.

"Well, did she?"

Sean said nothing. Sabrina watched him stare directly into the pale-blue eyes of his half brother, who was equally handsome but in a fair, Scandinavian way. Gavin had gelled the front of his hair in what she guessed was an effort to seem hipper and younger than his actual midforties. That was usually a sign that a guy had or was about to stray, something she'd come to realize too late after her own husband had started slicking his hair into a greasy tuft. Men were just so obvious.

"Are you kidding me? You need to get control over that woman or your marriage is going to feel like a life sentence without parole. She can't become a part of this family and stay in this company without a friggin' prenup." Gavin sounded more authoritative and angry than his father had.

"Sure she can. Watch," Sean said, turning away.

"Is your wife around or shall I go find her to make sure she knows brunch is about to be served?" Sabrina asked.

"What? Oh, she must be in the girls' room."

But Lisa Keating wasn't. The girls—Gavin and Lisa's daughters—refused to open their door until Sean explained he was just telling them about breakfast.

Emma, the oldest, finally opened the door partway. She was a nine-year-old version of her lovely mother—blue-eyed with silky, straight blonde hair. She explained that they hadn't seen their mother and couldn't go to breakfast until they did because she had made them promise not to leave the room without her.

"And I need her 'cause I'm scared," said a little voice behind Emma.

"Zoey, is that you, honey? It's Uncle Sean."

Zoey scooted out from behind Emma and ran to Sean, who picked her up into his arms.

"Why are you scared?" Sabrina asked, afraid that something else might be wrong but figuring she'd better find out.

"I heard screaming. First, I thought it was Mommy fighting with Daddy, but then I could hear it outside the window. It woked me up."

"It woked me up, too," said a third blonde beauty, who seemed to be older than Zoey but younger than Emma.

"Oh Victoria, you poor thing. Let Uncle Sean give you a big hug."

Sabrina suggested that the girls go and get dressed while she and Uncle Sean find their mom.

"She probably went for a run. Hey, maybe Elena went with her," Sean said, turning to Sabrina.

"Do you think that's where she is?" she asked once the girls had closed the door, picturing a runaway bride in her gown wearing running shoes.

"Could be. Lisa's kind of an exercise fanatic, really conscious about her weight. Gavin has a thing about fat women."

"Well, maybe they're together. Are they good friends?" Sabrina began opening the doors of the unoccupied guest rooms, which were reserved for guests staying over after the wedding. From the little Sabrina had seen of both women, Lisa was as warm and natural as Elena was cold and superficial. But Elena had been so passionate about not signing the prenup that Sabrina wondered if she had misjudged her. There was a reason Sabrina didn't have a lot of female friends. She didn't trust herself to be able to reliably distinguish the Lisas from the Elenas. That was why Henry had given her a chocolate lab puppy named Girlfriend. He'd told her that she had to start somewhere.

"They're cordial, but basically have nothing in common. Lisa's a wife and mother but hasn't worked since Emma was born. Gavin can be pretty demanding and makes sure she keeps the home front running as efficiently as he likes to think he runs the business. But I suppose they could have struck up a conversation if Elena was looking for another woman to talk to," Sean said, pulling the last of the empty doors shut with no sign of either woman.

Sabrina suggested that Sean check the bridal suite once more to see if Elena had returned. She doubted it but needed to find Henry to regroup. What she no longer doubted was that an eleventh villa had been a very bad idea.

Chapter Three

Sabrina joined Henry in the great room, where he was supervising the waitstaff. While the great room at Nirvana was larger and grander than any other Sabrina had seen, it lacked charm and felt more like a hotel lobby. Classic Caribbean great rooms were comfortable living rooms in which the natural environment of the outdoors was brought inside and incorporated in the design: small palm trees, stone walls, indoor fountains, flowering plants, and large open windows inviting in the sunshine and trade winds.

Most of the guests seemed to enjoy going out to the truck, where Amy and Erin bantered with them as they made their selections. The Sammy, with two eggs, bacon or sausage, and a cheese of the guest's choice on a home-made biscuit, seemed to be the biggest hit, followed by the Breakfast BLT.

"Any luck?" Henry asked.

Sabrina motioned for Henry to follow her into the kitchen, where guests wouldn't hear their conversation.

"Not unless you mean bad luck. Now we can't seem to find the sister-in-law either."

"Do you mean Lisa or Heather? Heather's in the great room having brunch with her father and the company CFO. I wouldn't blame Lisa for taking off from that bore for a husband, Gavin. What an egomaniac. But she's got those three girls, so she's probably just off for a morning walk."

"Run. Sean says she runs. Remind me, who's Heather?" Sabrina asked as she admired how professional the Ten Villas' waitstaff looked in their new party shoes. Sabrina had been horrified when her entire waitstaff showed up for the dry run of the wedding event in flip-flops in varying degrees of decay.

"You can't wear those to serve at a wedding. Come in shoes for the event," she'd told them. Except they didn't own shoes, which was common on St. John, where fancy flip-flops were as dressed up as people got. Ten Villas had to spring for twelve pairs of black Tevas at full price.

"Heather's Sean's half sister," Henry said, as if Sabrina should know this information. Sabrina could never keep the names of the guests coming to and leaving from Ten Villas straight without her notebook, although she remembered the details of everything else like Rain Man. Henry kept names all in his head like the manifests from his days as a flight attendant. Before things became so tense between them, they would joke that between the two of them they had a whole brain.

"Heather's a chiropractor from San Francisco. She's Kate Keating's daughter from marriage numero uno. Seems nice. Must look like her father," Henry said, diplomatically omitting the fact that Heather was not as attractive as her mother or half brother. Tall with broad shoulders and narrow hips, she had a masculine look, which was only underscored by her short, frizzy salt-and-pepper hair.

"No. No sign of Elena," Sean said, dashing into the kitchen, almost out of breath. Sabrina felt her sense of urgency growing. Two women missing. The prenup and the wedding seemed less important now.

"Henry, why don't you and Sean check downstairs and then meet me back here," Sabrina said, needing time to think. She knew Henry was counting on her to come up with Plan B if they couldn't locate Elena and, now, Lisa. He knew she was a survivor who always had an alternative plan in her back pocket. If Plan A didn't work, on to Plan B and down through the alphabet. Somehow, it didn't seem fair that Henry had insisted they add this eleventh villa to Ten Villas but expected her to bail him out now that the event seemed to be going up in flames. Even after their interview with Sean and Elena, when Sabrina had cautioned Henry that she had an immediate sense that Elena would be difficult to work for, he wouldn't listen. Then he had done worse. He had accused her of being jealous.

"Are you sure you're not just reacting to having to answer to a powerful woman because that's what you once were?"

He could have slapped her across the face and she would have been less shocked. But she also wondered if he was right. She had fallen off a skyscraper of disgrace.

Sabrina checked the clock on the kitchen wall. It was still early, she told herself. There was plenty of time to find Elena and Lisa and keep the wedding plans on track. And so far, other than the missing bride and her future sister-in-law, things were going well. Guests who were staying at either the Westin or Caneel Bay, the two island hotels, had begun to arrive for breakfast. The sound of jovial chatter came from the great room, where Sabrina returned to make certain things stayed on track.

Out of the corner of her eye, Sabrina saw Sean's mother, Kate Keating, practically power walking up the slight incline from the front drive. Kate was a wiry, thin woman in her sixties. Her thick, short white hair accented a tan face with just enough wrinkles to suggest she'd been smart enough to wear sunscreen. Kate looked older as she drew closer, almost sprinting toward Sabrina, who rushed forward to meet her.

"Mrs. Keating, are you all right?"

"Something is wrong. Really wrong. In the water."

Sabrina wondered if the next challenge of her day might be giving CPR to Kate Keating, who looked ready to faint. What could be wrong in the water that she would be so upset? She obviously hadn't been in the water. Her skirt and blouse were bone-dry other than what looked like little splattered drops of paint.

"What do you mean?"

"Come see for yourself." Kate pulled Sabrina by the hand, dragging her down the small hill at the bottom of the driveway, in the direction of Ditleff Point Beach. The small beach bordered a tiny cove, which was the only place to swim, launch a small boat, or paddleboard in the area. Arriving at the beach, Sabrina could see an easel sitting on the bluff above them.

Kate pointed out at the water to the right where waves rolled in, crashing against the jagged rocks that rose up from the sea in a gentle rhythm.

"I've been painting the waves all morning. I love how they slide in and over the rocks. They break into these white foamy lines that look like lace curtains blowing in a breeze," Kate said.

Sabrina nodded. That was exactly what she thought of when she watched those waves breaking. They reminded her of the white Irish lace curtains in Ruth's motel cottages back in Allerton, the coastal Massachusetts town where she'd grown up. Distracted by how uncanny it felt to hear someone else share the same impression, Sabrina was jarred back by the urgency in Kate's voice.

"Look. Can you see that the symmetry is off at the nearest point where the waves are breaking? There's something white moving with the waves but not in line with them. It doesn't break into foam like the rest of the waves do. Something's not right."

Sabrina scanned the area, looking from left to right and back again several times. She had watched the waves in this cove a thousand times, in the distance, from her tiny cottage up above on a hill in Fish Bay. It was Sabrina's form of meditation. Kate was right. Something was very wrong.

"Has it moved at all?" she asked.

"Just a little when a wave comes. I didn't notice it at first. I was filling in the clouds and sky when I started. Do you think it's a person? Maybe a dead shark?"

She was grateful Kate didn't know there were two women missing from Villa Nirvana. She knew once again she had the misfortune to stumble upon a situation that at the very least called for action. Oh, she could wait and send for help, but if that really was a person, people would want to know why she hadn't just done what needed to be done.

"I'm going to go out on the paddleboard and find out," Sabrina said, grateful that her boyfriend, Neil Perry, had given her one for her birthday the month before and that she had mastered it enough to at least not fall over much.

She kicked off her flip-flops, placed her cell phone and keys on top of one, and picked up the yellow paddleboard that was sitting on its side in a rack on the sand. She brought it down to the edge of the water.

"Kate, please hold the board so it doesn't float away," Sabrina said as she went back to the rack and grabbed a paddle.

The shallow water, having already been heated by the sun, felt warm on her feet. She pushed the board in until she was waist deep and climbed on, placing one knee down at a time. She moved to the center of the board and placed her hands in front of her, gradually raising her body to a standing position. She tucked her pelvis and gave a slight bend to her knees and reminded herself to breathe, just as if she were in mountain pose during yoga.

Normally, Sabrina would have moved toward the right where there were fewer rocks, but what she needed to explore was to the left. She hoped there was enough water between the rocks and coral that the board wouldn't scrape against them and topple her over. She paddled out, keeping her eyes on the surface of the water. Reaching the area where the waves were breaking, the paddleboard began to rock. No, standing was not going to work. She was going to have to use the board on her belly.

Sabrina bent at the waist, placed her hands back on the board and lowered herself onto her abdomen. Placing the paddle next to her, she began paddling with her hands toward what she could now see was a white object undulating with the surf about thirty feet away. Checking the depth of the water for clearance, she moved toward the object.

Sabrina could see the white lace moving on the top of the water, back and forth as the waves moved in and out. No one had to tell her she had found the missing bride.

Chapter Four

Sean led the way down the stone steps into the subterranean area of Villa Nirvana. Henry thought of it as "the Cave." Below ground level, there was a huge storage room, a cavernous wine cellar, a roomy media and business center, and a commercial kitchen that served as a food prep area. Henry checked the storage room while Sean ducked into the wine cellar and kitchen.

"Nothing," Henry said.

"A bottle of wine missing from the front rack, but no Elena."

They opened the door to the media room that had an enormous screen on one wall, which was now dimmed with the DVD menu to *Breakfast at Tiffany's* displayed. The glow of the screen fell on Lisa, asleep on the first of a collection of black leather couches and lounge chairs, curled up under a colorful, West Indian–style throw.

"One mystery solved," Henry said, hitting a light switch as Sean moved toward her and gently shook her shoulder.

"What? Oh my God, did I fall asleep? What time is it?" Lisa asked, springing to her feet as the throw fell to the floor, exposing her bare arms and fresh black-and-blue marks that Henry thought looked like thumbprints.

"Are you okay?" Sean asked.

"Of course," Lisa said, pulling the throw around her like a shawl. "I couldn't sleep, so I came down to watch a movie. I'd better get to the girls."

"They're waiting in their room so you can take them to breakfast. Did you happen to see Elena on your nocturnal travels?" Henry asked.

Lisa hesitated, looking from Henry to Sean.

"I can't find her, Lisa. I want to make it right," Sean said.

"She watched the movie with me for a while. We had a little girl talk, that's all."

"What was she wearing?" Henry asked.

"Her wedding gown. It's gorgeous. Very fifties, tea length. I told her to be careful not to spill the red wine, so she opened a bottle of champagne from the wine cellar and gave me the bottle of red she'd been drinking. Bad idea, I guess, because I'd already had plenty of wine on top of a Xanax earlier, when there was all that shouting over the prenup. That's probably why I slept until now. I've got to get going. Gavin will kill me when he finds out," Lisa said, moving toward the door.

"Do you know when Elena left?" Henry asked.

"Where did she say she was going?" Sean added.

"I don't know. I must have fallen asleep during the movie. We put *Breakfast at Tiffany's* on after our little chat. I told her it was a good movie if she needed to cry. I've seen it a gazillion times. I've never thought of Elena as emotional, but I guess canceling a wedding would do that to anyone."

Henry knew they needed to continue the search for Elena, and he also had to let Sabrina know they had found Lisa safe. But he sensed Lisa might know more than she was saying, or was even aware she knew.

"Did she actually say she was going to call it off?" Sean's voice cracked.

"Sean, I never thought I'd see you so crazy about a woman. I thought you'd never settle down. I'm sorry this has gotten so ugly for you. I told Elena she should just sign and have her beautiful wedding. I said after a few years and a couple of kids, she'd forget she even had a prenup. I know I have. Look, I've got to go. The girls are spending the day at the Westin with their grandmother after breakfast," Lisa said, placing her hand on the door handle.

"Wait, Lisa. What did she say to that?" Henry asked.

Lisa looked at Sean and then back at Henry.

"Go ahead, Lisa. Tell us. I brought this all on myself. You don't have to spare me," Sean said.

"She said I didn't understand. That you and she weren't going to have any kids. And that she wasn't signing any prenup." Lisa left, careful not to look at Sean as she walked by him.

Sean slumped into the nearest chair.

"Look, we still have time to find her. When you tell her you don't care about the prenup, everything will be fine. You'll see," Henry said, not sure if he believed what he was saying but knowing it was what Sean needed to hear.

"No, I've lost her. I know that for sure now."

"How? You can't be certain," Henry said.

"Henry, Elena and I had very specific plans for our life together. Neither of us have ever been married or in a committed relationship like this before. Everything we've decided has been intentional, with a lot of thought and discussion. It's what made me fall in love with Elena. She taught me to respect women as my equal. We were going to wait three years so Elena and I could continue to grow the business before my father's retirement. And then we were going to have two babies. We even had names picked out for them. No, I must have hurt her so badly, she couldn't forgive me."

Henry took the white linen hanky he always carried and handed it to Sean to wipe the tears that were rolling down his cheeks.

Chapter Five

The rocks had been deep enough below the surface for Sabrina to glide the paddleboard over them but were still high enough to snag the lace on the wedding gown Elena had drowned in. Sabrina knew Elena was dead, her limp, lifeless body floating and twirling in whichever direction the waves dictated. Should she try to bring the body back to shore? Was it possible she just had hypothermia and could be revived? She'd read countless stories about people surviving in water for hours. But wasn't that cold water? And hadn't most of those stories been urban legends? On some level, she knew she was thinking crazy.

Sabrina wasn't sure if she even could or should bring Elena back on the paddleboard, but if she didn't, somehow she would be blamed for what happened to her—just like she had been blamed for her husband's death and had been a person of interest in the death of a villa guest several months ago. No, Elena was getting on the paddleboard and going back.

Sabrina tugged at lace that was affixed to something below the water. The lace felt odd to the touch, almost scratchy. She pulled and pulled at what she imagined was the bottom of the skirt of the dress until she felt the resistance released. Next, she grasped Elena around the waist, grateful that Elena's long straight black hair was covering her face, and moved her toward the paddleboard, hoisting the tiny woman partially up on it.

Holding Elena with one arm and the board with the other, Sabrina flutter kicked them toward the shore. She kicked hard and fast, fueled by anger at the dead woman, who had killed herself over a man (something Sabrina couldn't understand), thereby inflicting trauma on the lives of everyone around her, including Sabrina. Why hadn't this shrewd businesswoman just dumped Sean and moved on? Why kill herself?

Kate ran into the water to help pull the paddleboard to shore.

"Oh dear God, it's Elena. My Sean will be devastated. Why would she do this?" Kate asked, kneeling beside the slumped pile of lace. Kate rolled Elena over on to her back and grabbed one of her wrists to feel for a pulse.

"I was a nurse before I married Jack. That's how I met him," Kate said, now reaching under Elena's hair to find her carotid artery, but not exposing the face neither of them wanted to see. Sabrina noticed bruises on Elena's neck. Several oval spots and then a linear mark. But she didn't want to think what the implications of that were.

She bent over, retching and coughing up salt water she didn't remember swallowing, knowing Kate was confirming that Elena was gone.

Sabrina found the flip-flop where she had left her cell phone and dialed 9-1-1, grateful for her new and improved relationship with Detective Leon Janquar, who had presented her with a certificate for heroism for saving a young woman's life. At least she knew the police wouldn't be hostile toward her this time and that they no longer blamed her for making the police in Nantucket look foolish when they investigated her husband's death.

She told the dispatcher who answered that there had been a drowning at the cove out on Ditleff Point Beach and to please let Detective Janquar know.

"Oh, he's not on today. He'll be out for the next month. He's having knee replacement surgery."

Chapter Six

Shivering in her wet clothes despite standing under the blast of the Caribbean sun, Sabrina saw she had a text message from Henry.

"Found L safe. No E. Think she's dumped S."

Sabrina looked over at Kate Keating, not knowing what to say. She decided the best thing she could do was clue Henry in and contain the situation.

"E drowned. Am at cove with Kate K. Keep S at house. Cops coming."

But it was too late, Sabrina realized. Lisa Keating, who was driving down the driveway with her three children, paused when she saw Kate and Sabrina standing at the top of the beach. She got out of the rental car, keeping the children waiting in the jeep with the air conditioning going and windows rolled up.

"What's going on, Kate? Is everything all right?" Sabrina wanted to tell Kate to say nothing, but she had already begun to sob, rushing up to Lisa's waiting arms.

"She'd dead, Lisa. Elena's dead. She drowned. In her wedding gown." Kate's sobs became howls so loud that the children could surely hear them, even with the windows up.

Lisa looked up at the car and then back at the beach past Sabrina, where all that could be seen was a pile of white lace. "Were you on your way to the Westin to drop off the girls with your mother?" Sabrina asked. Sabrina had an entire notebook filled with the itinerary and activities of all the family members staying at Villa Nirvana. She might not remember names as well as Henry, but once she wrote anything else in her notebook, she never forgot it. She knew the Keating girls were scheduled to spend the day with their grandmother until late in the afternoon, when they would return to be flower girls in the wedding.

Lisa stared at her without responding for a moment, reminding Sabrina that she must look frightful with her wet hair hanging in limp curls and soaked-through clothes.

"Yes, I mean no. I mean they're staying with Gavin's mother," Lisa said.

"Gavin's mother?" Sabrina looked at Kate puzzled. She'd assumed it would be Lisa's mother with the grandchildren over at the Westin.

"Gavin's mother decided to come to St. John to help with the children during the wedding weekend," Lisa said.

"A wedding to which she is not, was not, invited." Kate stopped sobbing for a moment. Sabrina took some comfort in hearing once again that hers was not the only screwed-up family. But she knew there was no time to waste on family politics if the Keating kids were to be spared the sirens and ambulance, paramedics, and cops. And there was just no reason for them to be exposed to what was about to ensue.

"Lisa, I'd hop in that jeep and get the kids out of here before—"

"You're right. Say no more. I'll be right back, Kate. I'm so sorry," Lisa said, rushing to the jeep and taking off just in time to miss the arrival of St. John Rescue and three cruisers.

With the sirens blasting, the vehicles raised enough dust from the dirt road leading to the cove and the Villa Nirvana driveway to make it difficult to see the faces of the people who had emerged from the villa to check out what was going on. Sabrina saw Sean race toward his mother. Henry followed close behind, giving Sabrina a look that said, "I couldn't hold him back."

"What's going on? Are you okay? Why are they here?" Sean asked as the rescue workers and cops surrounded Elena. Only then did he seem to comprehend that the situation did not directly involve Kate but centered on the person lying still on the beach.

Sabrina was relieved to see Lucy Detree, who had worked directly under Detective Janquar when Carter Johnson, a guest at Ten Villas, had been murdered several months before. The statuesque, young black officer was directing guests to move back to the house, including

Jack and Gavin Keating. Detree's name tag revealed that she'd been promoted to sergeant since Johnson's murder had been resolved. Sabrina hoped this was a sign that the newer, enlightened faction within the Virgin Island Police Department was making progress against the publicly denounced corrupt band of cronies that had ruined the reputation of the department.

"We own this villa, Officer. If there's an emergency on the premises, we are entitled to know what it is, in order to act accordingly," Gavin told Detree as he stepped around her, his father following right behind with Heather on his heels. Heather stepped up to Detree as the others were being guided back to the house by a uniformed officer.

"Officer, that's my mother," she said, pointing her finger over at Kate Keating. "I need to be there for her." She walked past Detree and over to Sean and Kate.

Kate had her arms around her son, who was sobbing like an inconsolable child. Heather walked over to them both and swept them into a huge hug.

"How can she be dead? She's supposed to get married in a couple of hours. I can't believe she would do this. How did it ever come to this?" Kate said, now joining Sean in sobbing, leaving Heather to comfort them both.

In the distance, guests who should have been arriving to join the brunch and island tour before the wedding were being turned away from the gatehouse. Guests who had already arrived had been ushered inside the villa, leaving Sabrina, Henry, and the immediate Keating family as the only people left at the beach, other than the rescue workers.

Jack and Gavin Keating approached Kate and her children. Somehow Sabrina suspected the circle of mourning wasn't wide enough to fit Gavin Keating. She wasn't sure about Jack.

"What's going on?" Gavin practically shouted over the crying.

"Elena is dead. It looks like suicide," Heather said.

"Oh no," Jack said, moving nearer to Kate, placing an arm on her shoulder.

"That's ridiculous. That can't be," Gavin said, sounding more insolent than incredulous.

Sean broke the circle and lurched toward Gavin with his fists ready for a fight. "What's ridiculous, you asshole? You know what's ridiculous? That you, more than anyone in the family, pressured Elena to sign that goddamn prenup, even though she made better decisions in the company in the six months she worked there than you did in the past six years. You're the reason she's dead. And me, because I didn't tell you to lay off."

"Are you saying she's really dead? That she killed herself?"

"What about dead don't you get, Gavin? Can't you even pretend to be a little sensitive at a time like this?" Heather said, raising her voice over her mother's sobs.

"Folks, I'm sorry about what's happened here, but I'm afraid you're all going to have to simmer down," a very deep voice bellowed. It came from a uniformed officer whose nameplate identified him as Detective Vernon Hodge.

"Fine. I'm out of here," Gavin said, turning to leave.

"Not so fast, sir. No one will be leaving for a while. We have a sudden and suspicious death of a young, seemingly healthy woman. The fact that she is wearing a bridal gown makes it all the more questionable. My men will be gathering information from each of you, so just follow Sergeant Detree back to the house and follow her instructions."

Sabrina watched Lucy Detree's jaw tighten at the sound of "my men."

Chapter Seven

Sabrina, Henry, and the Keating family were ushered by Sergeant Detree through the now-empty great room to a table that had been set up with four others under canopies around the pool. Sabrina had agonized over the details of how the tables should be placed and set so that everything would be perfect for the wedding at sunset. She'd had two practice sessions with the Ten Villa staff, who'd done a fine job setting up for the wedding banquet while Sabrina had been pulling the bride's body out of the water.

That Elena had chosen to fill the great room and pool area with two dozen potted gardenia bushes had not surprised Sabrina. There was no fussier nor more elegant flower than the gardenia. The cloud of fragrance that now filled Villa Nirvana screamed Elena's name. Her bridal bouquet and Sean's boutonniere, both made of gardenias, probably still sat in the extra refrigerator in the downstairs storage room, never to be worn by either. The tiny white diamond-like faerie lights, which would have sparkled around the perimeter of the pool and the edges of the canopies above the tables, would never be lit. As much as Sabrina found Villa Nirvana ostentatious and vulgar, it made her sad to know the miniature replicas of it, which sat in the center of each table, with a candle inside ready to be lit, would remain dark.

What a waste of time and energy. There would be no wedding banquet, no wedding. Her staff sat at another table, unusually quiet. Guests Sabrina didn't know were scattered at other tables. She recognized Paul Blanchard, the company CFO, sitting alone at one. He'd been the only person invited to stay overnight at Villa Nirvana after the rehearsal dinner that Sabrina had yet to meet.

"I'd prefer to wait in my room," Gavin told Sergeant Detree, once again attempting to bypass her.

"I don't care what you prefer, sir. This is the scene of a police investigation and must be treated as such," Detree said. Gavin turned around and found a seat next to Paul Blanchard, rather than join the immediate family.

"At least let Sabrina get into some dry clothes and comb that mop of hair," Henry said. He was always after Sabrina to tame her full head of shoulder-length curls. He had known her when her smooth hairstyle and chic clothes were provided by a television studio. Sabrina, on the other hand, loved that she no longer owned a hair dryer and that she dried her hair by driving with the windows open.

Detree agreed to let Sabrina change, but not inside the house or in the cabana, which had dressing rooms just for this purpose. Sabrina had to slip behind the rental jeeps and duck down for privacy as she threw on the generic black shift she wore to pick guests up at the ferry.

She returned to the table where Henry sat with Sean, Kate, Jack, and Heather.

"I've texted Neil to come over." Henry leaned close to her ear as she sat down in one of those god-awful folding white chairs everyone thinks looks so darling in wedding pictures but is really like sitting on a sawhorse. She had tried to convince Elena to choose more comfortable chairs for the wedding, but the bride had preferred to make decisions based upon aesthetics.

Sean cocked his head in their direction. "Neil Perry? I did the same."

"You texted Neil? Why? How do you know him?" Sabrina asked. She was occasionally uncomfortable with how little she really knew about the man many island friends considered her boyfriend, including her, at times. She had spent so much time denying her attraction to Neil that when she finally succumbed to his charm, his history seemed irrelevant. After several months of spending plenty of time together (mostly evenings after work when they would take a swim with Sabrina's dog, Girlfriend, then share a meal and sometimes more), Sabrina had grown comfortable with Neil and their routine.

But just recently, he had grown somewhat distant, like the night before when she knew he had to fill in for one of the bartenders at Bar None, the beach bar he owned.

She'd offered to bring home some of the leftover tapas from the rehearsal dinner. Just a few weeks before, Neil would have been eager to come sit on her porch after work, sipping a nightcap, munching on leftovers. But last night, he'd said he'd prefer just to go home to his place once he was done with his late shift. Just when she had let her guard down and begun to trust him, he seemed preoccupied, and it felt like he was retreating. Sabrina started to wonder if she was going to get dumped again.

"He was my lawyer in LA," Sean said, as if Sabrina should know this.

"Is he coming?" Henry asked.

"I don't know. I got his voicemail. I know he can't actually practice law here, but I like and trust Neil. He's got common sense, which is why I went to talk to him at Bar None last night. I thought maybe he could help me with the prenup problem," Sean began to choke up. Kate reached over and took his hand.

"Isn't he the one whose office building you bought when he wanted to leave town fast and move here?" Jack asked.

"Yeah, then we tore it down and made a bundle when we built a parking garage. I wish I'd gotten to talk to him last night. Maybe then none of this would have happened, but he had taken off to pick up some woman."

He had taken off to pick up some woman? Sabrina had been right. He had been backing off. Why didn't he just say he was no longer interested? She wasn't one of those clingy women who couldn't let go. Sabrina might have been caught off guard when she discovered her husband, Ben, had been cheating on her. But Ruth, the woman who had raised her, had taught her a few lessons about life and one of them was, "Fool me once, shame on you. Fool me twice, shame on me." Neil Perry would not get the opportunity to make a fool of her. He was now history. She had a full life and a business to run, which at this point was likely in trouble with the second suspicious death of a guest at one of her villas in just a few months. She needed to get her act together. She needed not to cry in front of these people.

Sabrina leaned over to speak to Henry privately.

"We need to do something about canceling the dinner from Zeus and the music."

"We also need to find a place for the Keating family to stay. The other island hotels are already full with the other wedding guests," Henry said.

Gavin strutted over to the table, holding out his smartphone. Looking directly at Jack Keating, he began reading from his phone.

"Keating Construction sadly announces the death of one of its most valuable employees, Elena Consuela Soto Rodriguez. Ms. Rodriguez appears to have drowned accidentally during a company event. The Keating family requests their privacy be respected during this difficult time."

Gavin put his phone in his pocket while everyone sitting at the table gaped at him without speaking. Why would Gavin have written a statement at all, let alone one that was so misleading?

"Are you kidding?" Sean finally asked.

"Jack, please tell Gavin not to release any statement until we've all had a chance to discuss it. This is premature, inaccurate, and totally inappropriate," Heather said.

"Too late. I've already released it. It's called damage control. You have to take a situation like this by the balls or it will have you by yours. You should know that, Heather," Gavin said.

"You are just compounding a family misfortune, Gavin. I can't believe you've managed to make this terrible tragedy worse than any of us could imagine," Kate said.

"Well, you don't have to imagine it getting any worse now, Mother. Look who just walked through the door," Heather said, pointing to a thin, blonde older woman dashing ahead of Lucy Detree, who was clearly trying to catch up with her.

"Who's that?" Henry asked, but Sabrina had already guessed.

"That's Anneka Lund Keating. My ex-wife," Jack said, shaking his head.

Chapter Eight

Neil Perry checked the messages on his mobile phone. The new bartender he'd hired was available to fill in again for the evening shift. Mark Wentworth had been a godsend the night before when Neil got the call from Cassie Thomas about an accident. Neil was filling in for his regular bartender, Mitch. The other two bartenders were off sailing for the weekend. Mark had done a good job, and Neil was grateful he'd hired him.

Larry Thomas had taken the corner right before Bordeaux Mountain a little too sharply. His jeep jettisoned off the road and down twenty feet into a patch of rain forest. The vegetation was so thick that if someone hadn't been driving behind him, Larry might not have been found for days.

St. John Rescue had to use the Jaws of Life to get him out of his jeep and bring him to the Myrah Keating Smith Health Center. Cassie asked if Neil would pick her up and take her to the clinic since Larry was driving their only vehicle.

Of course he would, as soon as he found coverage for the bar. Larry was a good customer and friend. He ran the only seaplane out of St. John and had taken Neil to a number of islands when he first moved from LA.

He hadn't expected that Larry would be dead on arrival. Apparently neither had Cassie, who totally lost it and needed Neil to stay with her while she summoned her closest girlfriends. He didn't want to have to comfort and console her while they waited, but he did. Wasn't this one of the main reasons he had gotten out of practicing law? Too much human misery. And when it found him personally, packaged first in a divorce and then in the death of his only son, he'd gotten out fast, selling everything and moving to paradise. Paradise. Right.

If the two messages on his phone—both urgent—were an indication of how his life in paradise was going to be today, he ought to just buy a one-way ticket back to LA. Or break down and just take the frigging Virgin Islands bar exam.

The voicemail from an old client didn't surprise him. Mark had told him that Sean Keating had stopped by Bar None the night before. What did surprise him was the message itself. Sean's fiancée had died out on Ditleff Point, a remarkable coincidence because he knew Sabrina and Henry had a huge wedding at the new villa out there.

Henry's text had been more cryptic. "Death on Ditleff. Sabrina and I need you here NOW. Please."

Sabrina Salter, known to Neil as "Salty," which drove her a little crazy, was the woman he found himself falling in love with. How could she be involved in another death? Only a few months before, she'd needed help from Neil with a police investigation for a similar incident. He didn't think she did anything intentional to attract these situations any more than he did anything to encourage people to constantly seek his help.

Neil looked at the open bar review book. Commercial Paper. He had hated studying the Uniform Commercial Code thirty years before when he was preparing to take the California bar exam. Dry and boring then, and no less so now. The US Virgin Islands had no reciprocity, regardless of how long you had practiced law anywhere. But the way things were going, if he didn't take the bar exam, he ran the risk of being accused of practicing law without a license. No one, not even Salty, knew he was even considering putting himself through the ordeal of sitting for the bar exam again.

He didn't have to do this to himself. If he wanted to practice law again, he could go back to California. His ticket was still good. The amount of business his name alone would bring in would make any firm want to hire him.

Go back? What was he thinking? Was it just all this tugging at his sleeve for help that was making him crazy?

He loved living in St. John, on an old Bristol trawler in Coral Bay where he had to either row or paddle to get home.

He slammed the bar review book closed. There were people who needed him. He thought of poor Larry Thomas, who had run out of choices the night before, and decided agonizing over his own was a privilege.

Chapter Nine

Sitting under the shade of the canopied table, Sabrina watched Lucy Detree catch Anneka Lund Keating by the elbow just as the woman reached their table. She marveled at how Anneka's branch of the family made a perfect blonde brigade, starting with its matriarch and extending down to the fair grandchildren.

She was grateful that Henry had suggested to Sean that they move away from the family table to find better reception for their phones and see if they'd heard from Neil. Sean didn't need to be provoked by anyone else. He'd been on an emotional roller coaster since the night before, and Gavin had nearly unraveled him twice in the last half hour.

"Ma'am, you are not the Mrs. Keating we requested return for questioning. We are looking for Lisa Keating," Sergeant Detree said as Anneka shook her arm free of the police officer's hold.

"Well, you people should communicate more clearly then. I gave my name at the gate and they let me come right in. Since I'm here, I need to make sure my son is all right. Gavin, dear, this is just awful." Anneka waltzed over to peck his cheek.

"It's unfortunate, but I think I've got things in control, at least as far as the business goes," Gavin said.

"Officer, please remove this woman from the premises. She has no business being here. We are grieving the loss of a woman who should be marrying our son this evening. We need our privacy," Kate Keating said, standing to face Lucy Detree. Heather rose and stood next to her mother.

"For the love of God, Anneka, can you just let it go for once?" Jack said, not standing to join the warring women.

Detree seemed frozen after witnessing the family spar. Sabrina had had enough. She rose to her feet and pulled Detree to the side.

"There's some bad blood in this family. I think this situation could get a lot worse if the wrong Mrs. Keating, who by the way was the first Mrs. Keating, doesn't leave quickly. I hope you don't mind me cluing you in."

"Got it. Thanks."

"Come now or I'll have to arrest you, ma'am. This is an official police investigation." Detree grabbed Anneka by the same arm she'd grasped while attempting to stop her just minutes before.

"Mother, I'm fine. Go watch the girls, please," Gavin said, seeming to comprehend that his mother was on the verge of incarceration. Sabrina remained standing behind Sergeant Detree, staring at mother and son. She was reminded of the old saying about the apple not falling far from the tree.

Anneka glared back at Sabrina, then smirked.

"Aren't you that weather reporter who murdered her husband?" Looking over her shoulder at Kate and Jack, she said, "You people really know how to throw a wedding."

Chapter Ten

Neil arrived at Villa Nirvana just in time to see an older blonde woman being escorted out by Sergeant Lucy Detree.

"Hey, Lucy, what you got going here?" Neil asked the young policewoman he'd met through Detective Janquar.

"Sorry, Neil. This is an official police investigation. Can't talk about it." Lucy slammed the door to Anneka's rental car shut.

"I'm here officially. I got a call from a client I represented in LA that his fiancée died here. I'm here to help him out until I can find local counsel for him," Neil lied. Why did he think he'd be reading more about Commercial Paper the way things were going?

"Oh, you mean Sean Keating? In that case, come on up to the house. We've got everyone sitting around the pool. Don't go anywhere else. We haven't started in the house."

Neil's legal antennae popped at the sound of Lucy's warning. This sounded more like a criminal investigation to a seasoned criminal lawyer.

"Are people free to leave?" Neil asked. He knew the rules on paper regarding criminal procedure in the islands were not the same as those practiced. He hoped they were as loose as usual.

"We're letting the people who didn't arrive until this morning for the brunch go shortly. They all have their names on a list at the gatehouse showing their arrival times so they can be ruled out. Except your girlfriend and her partner. They get to stay and give statements with the other people who were here last night when it appears the death occurred."

Neil caught a ride up to the house with Detree. He paused at the foot of the driveway, taking in the sheer ostentatiousness of the villa.

He could see Amy and Erin were packing up the Triple B food truck. The open great room, which served as the center of the house, was empty other than for a few cops with purple gloves standing around, a sign the cops were collecting evidence. At the far end of the great room was the predictable infinity pool, although this one even had a fancy fountain. He spotted Sabrina and Sean at one of the tables around the pool.

Neil strode confidently toward them, not acknowledging the cops in the great room. Oh, he still knew how to play this game. The question was, did he want to?

Sean saw him first, getting up from his chair where he'd been sitting next to Henry. Sean rushed toward him, hand stretched out, ready to greet him.

"Neil, thanks for coming. Things are a mess here."

Neil shook Sean's hand, remembering how he'd saved his butt from a drunk and disorderly charge that had involved the daughter of a film director and had promised to get ugly. He'd helped Sean out a few other times for a few misdemeanors that weren't uncommon with young men in their twenties who drink too much and think getting laid is a national sport. But he'd liked Sean and remembered how he'd come up with quick cash when Neil wanted out of LA fast.

Neil walked back with Sean to the table, saying hello to Sabrina and Henry after being introduced to Jack and Kate Keating and Heather Malzone.

"What did you find out? They're not telling us anything," Sabrina jumped in.

"How about first someone clues me in?" Neil asked, not entirely sure he actually wanted to know.

"They're not saying whether Elena committed suicide, Neil. We were supposed to be married here this evening. She wouldn't sign the prenup my family wanted to protect the business. She felt we were attacking her character. I was so stupid. I went to tell her I didn't care about the pre-nup this morning, but she was gone," Sean said. "She was the one, Neil. You know what I mean? The real thing."

Neil looked at Sabrina without even thinking. But she looked away from him and stared at her phone.

"I thought she was distraught over the prenup and that she'd committed suicide, but the police have been treating us like something criminal has happened ever since Sabrina brought Elena in on the paddleboard," Kate said.

"You went out and got the body, Salty? Really?" Whatever was she thinking? Why didn't she just wear a T-shirt that said, "Dead bodies find me"? Neil figured the bar exam was definitely a good idea if Salty was in his future.

"Kate spotted her while she was painting. We couldn't tell what we were seeing floating in the water. If I didn't check and Elena was alive and then drowned, everyone would have blamed me. You know that, Neil."

"Calm down, Salty," Neil reached to pat her hand, but Sabrina drew it away. This was way more than he'd bargained for when he dropped everything to come help.

"Calm down? Don't you dare tell me to calm down, Neil Perry. How condescending. I leap into action, ready to help in the best way I can, struggle to bring Elena in from the water, where the lace on her wedding gown had gotten stuck on a rock—"

"She was in her wedding gown?" Neil asked. He knew he had ignited Sabrina's temper and needed to apologize fast, but he couldn't get past the poor woman drowning in her wedding gown.

"Yes. It was an awful way to find her. Sabrina did a great job. I'm very grateful," said Kate, looking over at Sabrina, whose cheeks were still flushed from her outburst.

"Look, Salty, I'm sorry. I just can't wrap my head around all of this."

"She had it on late last night before we left Villa Nirvana. I went to see her before Sabrina and I left after clearing up after the rehearsal dinner. She had refused to sign the prenup and told me she may as well get to wear it because it didn't look like there was going to be a wedding," Henry chimed in.

"This really does sound more like suicide. Did anyone look for a note?" Neil asked.

Jack, Kate, and Sean all looked at one another like they'd been poked with a cattle prod.

"Neil, we haven't been allowed to do anything other than sit at this table. The cops barely let me get into dry clothes. They're treating the Keatings like they're criminals rather than a family who has just suffered a tragedy," Sabrina said.

Neil had been so focused on talking to Sabrina and the Keating family that he hadn't noticed everyone had left the other tables, including the waitstaff from Ten Villas, with the exception of two men sitting several tables away.

"Who are those two guys?" Neil asked.

"My other son, Gavin, and the company CFO, Paul Blanchard," Jack said.

"Have the cops come over and told you not to discuss the case with anyone?" Neil asked.

Everyone shook their heads.

"Good. Let's chat a little before they're on to us."

Chapter Eleven

Sabrina's heart warmed at the huskiness in Neil's voice inviting all of them to have a chat. She was grateful for his presence and willingness to become involved, regardless of what happened to their personal relationship. He could be maddening, but there was something comforting about Neil. He had a sense of confidence that suggested he would get to the bottom of whatever it was. No big deal. We'll get it fixed. Sabrina was more worried about her business's reputation than being the person who found the body, but she still didn't like being this close to another investigation. She hoped there would be a resolution long before anyone in the press connected Elena's death to her name.

She knew it would always be like this. She carried her own story like a string of tin cans tied to a car bumper after a wedding. She hadn't meant to kill Ben when she'd fled to their Nantucket vacation home after learning he was cheating on her. How was she to know he'd pick the same night—in the middle of the freakin' winter, no less—to bring his bimbo to their summer home? She'd thought there was a burglar in the house when she heard those noises and used Ben's own gun to fend off an intruder.

Except it wasn't an intruder. It had been her husband, and Sabrina had been tried for first-degree murder. Though acquitted, she lost everything she had scrambled so hard to earn. Her job as a Boston television meteorologist, her home on Beacon Hill, and most importantly, her privacy. Tabloid television featured her case every night for nearly two years.

Crime fighter and INN (In News Network) television host Faith Chase had tried to reignite the case against Sabrina a few months before when a villa guest had been murdered and Sabrina had discovered the body. She'd enlisted Neil's help with that case and hoped that if they were as successful working together on this one, she and Ten Villas would escape unscathed from this event. Sabrina knew she was stuffing her personal feelings for Neil down deep inside her, a survivor's skill she had learned as a child when she constantly had to explain the absence of her mother and had to live with the unpredictability that life with an alcoholic father brought. When you are always living on the edge, emotions become a luxury you can't indulge.

"Listen, folks, I'm happy to help you out here as much as I can, but you know I don't practice law anymore. I can maybe help you sort through some of this and then make a couple of calls to local counsel if you think you want or need representation. Do you mind if I ask a few questions?"

When no one objected, Neil jumped right in.

"When is the last time each of you saw Elena alive? Sean, you go first."

"Last night when I went to her room to ask her one more time if she wouldn't just sign the prenup to keep my family happy. I told her I would never enforce it. She threw me out of the room," Sean said, shaking his head as if he couldn't believe he had pushed the issue so far. "That's when I drove over to Bar None to see if you were there, Neil. It had to be after eleven thirty."

"How about the rest of you?" Neil opened it up to the group.

"When she stormed out of the great room and went up into her room, I followed and tried reasoning with her once more. But she wouldn't open her door, so I talked through it and just asked her to think about the big picture. I mean, it isn't as if anyone thought the marriage would fail. It was just a precaution. I told her I had signed one," Kate said.

"Same here, but when I knocked on her door and she told me to go away, I did. Don't get me wrong, I liked Elena, but she wasn't warm and fuzzy like Lisa. She was a businesswoman, and I was done arguing with her. I came back down and Kate and I hit the sack," Jack said.

Sabrina was surprised to find she felt sorrier for the Keatings than for Elena. It sounded like they were blindsided by Elena's last-minute hysteria over signing the prenup. She made a note to ask Neil more about prenups once they had an opportunity to talk alone.

"I didn't see her after she left the great room. I wasn't about to try and persuade her to sign something she was so obviously opposed to. Isn't that like duress?" Heather asked Neil.

"Well, it can be. Prenups are contracts, but they have some added requirements and protections because they're between people who have a personal relationship with one another. It's not an arm's length transaction, like it is when you have a business contract. How about you, Henry? When did you last see Elena?"

Sabrina knew Henry wasn't happy with this question, as it was a source of discord between the two of them. They would eventually need to sort through the issues the eleventh villa had brought to their business relationship and friendship, but first things first.

"A little after eleven. Just before we left the villa. I felt bad for her. I mean, here she is on the night before her wedding and everyone keeps pushing a bunch of papers under her nose to sign. I went to her room. She had her dress on, with the train wrapped around her shoulders like a shawl. Her shoes were like the glass slippers out of Cinderella. She was obviously sad."

Sean let out a groan and put his head on his folded arms on the table.

Out of the corner of her eye, Sabrina saw Detective Hodge approaching. The tall, slender man strutted with confidence toward the table.

"Mr. Perry, Sergeant Detree tells me you're here to see a client. Might I ask when you got a license to practice law in the Virgin Islands, sir?"

Neil stood and rose, meeting Hodge eye to eye.

"Detective Hodge, good to see you again. You're certainly a busy man these days," Neil said, extending his hand. Hodge looked at it, then shook it quickly.

"About my question, sir."

"I represented Mr. Keating, Sean Keating that is, when I practiced in LA. I'm only here until we can find him local counsel," Neil said. Sabrina could feel Neil's discomfort. She felt uneasy, too. Why was this cop worried about an attorney being present at the request of a man whose bride had just drowned? Who cares where Neil was licensed? They weren't in court.

"Mr. Perry, you don't need me to lecture you about the danger of practicing law without a license, do you? It's one thing for you to be a Good Samaritan and bring the widow of a car accident victim to the clinic last night, but you will not be tolerated stepping over the line into areas reserved for professional law enforcement."

"Detective Janquar didn't have any problems when Neil helped with the Carter Johnson case," Sabrina couldn't resist pointing out the obvious discrepancy. Car accident. Victim. Widow. Wait a minute, Sabrina realized, an awful lot had happened on St. John in the last twenty-four hours.

"Wait. Who died in a car accident?" she asked, afraid of the answer. In the short time she'd lived on the island, Sabrina had come to know and care about many of its residents.

"Larry Thomas. He took the curve at Bordeaux too hard," Neil said.

Sabrina had just about had it. Screw this villa. The hell with its suicidal bride. Poor Larry Thomas, who flew sea planes just about every day of his life, died because he didn't navigate a curve right? And what was wrong with her, immediately indicting Neil as a cheater when he was only acting as a friend to a woman whose husband had just died?

"Look, if you want to question me, do it now. Otherwise, I'm leaving. I'm happy to talk to you or Sergeant Detree, but I have a caterer and music to cancel, and accommodations to find for these people, Detective," Sabrina said, standing up to face Hodge.

"Actually, Ms. Salter, you all need to leave. The EMTs have suggested that there are signs Ms. Rodriguez's death may not have been accidental or a suicide. Of course, we won't know for certain until the medical examiner does an autopsy over on St. Thomas. We have the dive and scene-of-the-crime teams on their way. None of you are permitted to leave the island, except you, Mr. Perry, because you have nothing to do with this case. Please leave your telephone numbers with Sergeant Detree and let the station know where you'll be staying once arrangements are made. Several of the safari taxi drivers who apparently were meant to take people on tours are waiting to take you where you need to go. No one is permitted to take anything," Vernon Hodge said in a voice devoid of any emotion except, Sabrina detected, a note of condescension.

"Are you saying Elena may have been murdered?" Sean lurched out of his chair, tipping it over.

"That's exactly what I'm saying, and why we'll be wanting to talk to you, your family, and the villa rental staff a whole lot more." Hodge crossed his muscular arms over his chest, clearly a signal for Sean to come no closer. Sabrina was relieved to see Neil place a hand on Sean's shoulder, knowing any confrontation with the police would only complicate matters. She remembered seeing marks on Elena's throat when Kate was checking for a pulse and was afraid she knew where this was heading.

"Let's head to the taxis, folks, so we can find you new accommodations." Sabrina gestured for the Keating entourage to follow her, but none of them moved.

"That's ridiculous. Who would want to kill Elena?" Kate sat shaking her head, leaning into Jack, who was seated next to her.

"That's what we're going to find out, ma'am." Hodge's thin lips curled at the corners of his mouth into the hint of a smile.

"Please walk out to the taxis now. Oh, and Ms. Salter. Don't worry about canceling the caterer. My people will be working here all night and will naturally need some fortification."

Chapter Twelve

Within three minutes, they were all herded into two taxis. Henry and Gavin got into one, which would drop them at the Ten Villas van parked on Gifft Hill outside of Henry's condo. Henry would then drive Gavin to the Westin, where he could be reunited with Lisa and his daughters at his mother's unit.

Sabrina was pleased at how quickly she and Henry had been able to pull a plan of sorts together. They'd worked together so well when establishing Ten Villas that Sabrina had been surprised by their conflict over whether to add Villa Nirvana to their roster. Now she felt they were back in sync again and could manage this crisis unified.

She and the remainder of the Keating family plus the company CFO were now headed in the second taxi to Ten Villas' only vacant house. Villa Bella Vista was located high atop Bordeaux Mountain, the highest point on St. John. Deep in the rainforest, Bordeaux had a mystical feel to it. Driving under the heavy shelter of locust, hog plum, and yellow prickle trees, climbing nearly to the peak to arrive at Bella Vista, Sabrina always felt as if she had entered the world of the fairy tales of her youth. Surely, this was the land of Hansel and Gretel.

The Keating clan sat in silence as Sabrina made phone calls along the way. Zeus restaurant would deliver some of the food to Villa Nirvana to keep Detective Hodge and his crew happy, but the remainder would be brought to Bella Vista, where she and Henry could at least feed the miserable Keatings. Henry would join her after dropping off ghastly Gavin, as Sabrina was beginning to think of him. He would also grab the lost-and-found pile and bring it along for the family.

Sabrina had been ready to chuck the pile of clothing and other items guests had left behind and didn't want to pay to have shipped back to them, but Henry's experience with the airlines paid off again. "Are you kidding me? Do you know how often we'll have guests arrive who will have had the airlines lose their luggage? They'll be thrilled with a few togs to see them through until their bags have been located or they can go shopping."

Pulling into the shaded circular driveway, Sabrina was surprised to hear the sound of splashing. The villa was supposed to be vacant. She knew it had been cleaned the day before after a party of eight returned home to Toronto, so there shouldn't be any Ten Villa staff present. Besides, she'd put everyone on duty at the wedding extravaganza.

While the Keatings disembarked from the taxi, Sabrina strode up the walkway, which was bordered on each side by shaded gardens, took her keys off her belt, and opened the door to the large great room with its cathedral ceiling. She continued to walk through toward the French doors at the rear of the room that led to the pool overlooking the British Virgin Islands. The majestic view was so incredible that she had often thought it unreal.

But the view she was treated to at that moment wasn't quite as majestic, nor was it unreal—two plentiful, bare white asses bounding out of the pool, heading through the gate and onto a path, which eventually led back to the road.

"What the hell was that?" Sean asked, coming up behind Sabrina.

"Oh dear lord," Kate said.

"I told you we should have kept our business on the mainland, Jack" Paul Blanchard sounded tired and grouchy.

"For once, I feel shapely," Heather said, chuckling.

Sabrina didn't bother trying to chase the duo, one female and the other clearly male from the sight of his bouncing parts, even from the rear. Why did this lunacy have to happen today? But maybe some comic relief was just what was needed.

"Meet the skinny-dippers, folks. They check out the villa rental schedules online to see which are occupied and hit the pools where no one is staying and skinny-dip, or as some have said, 'chunky-dunk.' No one knows who they are and it's driving everyone crazy. I'll bet they left their signature," Sabrina said, coming closer to the pool and pointing to a floating red hibiscus.

Normally, this would be when Sabrina would show guests around the home and help them with their luggage. But there was no protocol for what to do when guests were displaced from a villa where a murder had occurred. She had no food to offer, but she was sure there was a stash of alcohol in the bar left over from the previous guests. There always was. You just never knew what it would consist of. Definitely time to offer drinks, although it could hardly be called "happy hour."

"Can I offer everyone a drink while we wait for the food to arrive?"

No one declined, so Sabrina played bartender, fixing the drinks with what she had on hand. She was delighted to find decent scotch and vodka along with the usual vacationer's choices: banana rum, guavaberry vodka, and anything Kenny Chesney had ever been reported to sip while on island.

"Please join us, Sabrina," Kate said.

"Of course. You've had a difficult day too, dear," Jack said.

Sabrina poured herself a stiff vodka on the rocks, not missing the lemon slice she normally insisted on. Sabrina had never sat in the late afternoon sun in the great room of Bella Vista. She rarely sat in any of the Ten Villas, always preoccupied with details related to their guests' arrivals and departures. Now she could appreciate the design of the house, the subtlety of the deep-mahogany-trimmed walls coupled with couches and chairs covered with contrasting shades of green plant prints that gave the impression you were sitting in the cool of a garden, even as the last of the tropical sun beat down through the skylights. Sitting in a chair opposite Paul Blanchard, she realized they hadn't been formally introduced.

"Mr. Blanchard, I know this is a little late, but I'm Sabrina Salter. We were never actually introduced. I only met the family."

"Oh, but I am family. Jack and I are first cousins," Paul said, after taking a slug of Scotch half the size of the tumbler.

"Our mothers were sisters," Jack said, sounding like the drink was doing its magic.

This, Sabrina realized, was an opportunity for her to learn more about the Keating family and, more importantly, Elena. If it were true that Elena had been murdered, it would mean Sabrina had the misfortune of finding two homicide victims within several months, which not only would be bad for business but also might make her a target in the media. She needed to learn more about the people in Elena's life so she could fit the pieces together and figure out how and why she was killed. She had learned from her experience when Carter Johnson was murdered that tiny pieces of information join together to form a mosaic that would eventually lead to the killer.

The sun was fading and would soon begin to set, which would probably remind Sean about the wedding that should be taking place. Sabrina needed to engage the family in conversation quickly before he became emotional again. Neil was so slick at getting information out of people that they never realized they were divulging what they thought were their well-kept secrets. Henry was a little less adroit, but his directness had a charm of its own. Sabrina didn't think she had the social skills to seduce information from these people, who had far more poise than she could ever hope for. But she plunged in any way.

"Sean, I really haven't had a chance to say how sorry I am about what happened to Elena. This must be awful for you. I only met her a few times, so I don't really know what she was like," Sabrina said, feeling guilty for her disingenuousness. She could see Kate glancing at Sean to monitor his reaction. Sometimes it helped people to talk about lost ones.

"Smartest woman I ever met. But she's the one who taught me that brains are not enough. You have to have vision, too. That's what I needed help with. Hell, before her, I was just trying to find prime locations where Keating Construction could build parking garages with as many spaces as could fit. They had about as much charm as stacked plastic ice cube trays. Elena asked tough questions. Did I want parking garages to be my legacy? I never even thought about having a legacy until her."

"There's nothing wrong with building parking garages, Sean. People need places to park their cars, right,

Jack?" Paul said, emptying his tumbler and heading over to the bar to help himself to a refill.

"Yes, we've made a damn good living building garages. But Elena did bring some fresh thinking to the company, including recognizing the tax advantages of moving our headquarters from San Francisco to St. Thomas," Jack said.

"She was brilliant. She went to Babson undergraduate and Harvard Business School for her MBA. Here I was, barely able to get out of Golden Gate University with an undergraduate degree. I couldn't believe she was interested in me. We were so lucky when she decided to join the company," Sean said. Sabrina took his empty glass with hers and headed to the bar for refills.

"I think she was the lucky one," Heather said. "You're smart, adorable, and totally charming, baby brother. No, Elena was getting herself a good deal between you as a husband and becoming a permanent part of the company."

"Those are really great schools she attended. Babson and Harvard Business. I'm from Boston originally, and I know you don't get better than that. I couldn't help but hear she came from a poor childhood in Puerto Rico. She must have gotten good scholarships," Sabrina said, marveling that she was actually getting information. She needed to find out as much as possible about Elena so this story would be over before it ever got out and hot.

"She did. She grew up in the Louis Llorens Torres *caserio*, the absolute worst project in Puerto Rico. When she was a teenager, Elena's family died in an explosion set off by some drug lords after a deal with someone in her building went sour. The only reason she escaped was that she was staying with a classmate in another part of the *caserio* doing a school project. She said that if she hadn't been orphaned in that fire, she never would have gotten the scholarship to a private girls' academy, which ended up being her ticket to Babson and beyond," Sean said, accepting his refilled glass back from Sabrina.

"Maybe we can establish a scholarship fund in her memory, dear," Kate said softly.

"Of course we can. That would be a lovely tribute," Jack said, in an obvious effort to comfort his grieving son.

Sean stood and rushed over to the French doors, which overlooked the tropical shade garden at the front of the house. He pulled open the glass doors, letting the fragrance from the jasmine and gardenia plants rush in.

"But I don't want to start a scholarship fund. I want to be standing in this sunset at Villa Nirvana marrying Elena. I don't want her to be dead. I don't ever want to see another sunset without her," Sean said, bending over in a wail that Sabrina felt in her chest.

Kate and Jack rushed to Sean, each taking one of his arms.

"Let me show you a room where Sean can lie down and get some rest," Sabrina said, rising to lead them off to the bedroom closest to the great room. The sound of a sobbing man suffering a permanent sunset filled her ears and heart as the real sun sank below the horizon.

Chapter Thirteen

Henry cursed under his breath when he saw that he and Gavin had drawn a lime-green safari cab named "Mr. Terrific," driven by the most obnoxious cab driver on island, which was quite a distinction given the tight competition. Cutthroat, aggressive, and rude, cab drivers seemed to learn their manners from tourists and then some.

"Good afternoon," Henry greeted Mr. Terrific with the customary greeting on island. "Hi" and even "hello" were not considered proper. "Good morning," "good afternoon," "good day," and "good evening" were what worked on St. John. Mr. Terrific didn't bother to respond. Gavin skipped the greeting part all together.

Two miles later, Henry emerged from the back of the cab at Trade Wind Estates.

"Thank you," Henry said, stepping down from the open-air seat.

"That will be fifteen dollars," Mr. Terrific said.

"We already paid you in advance," Henry started toward the gate to his condo community.

"That was for the island tour. This was a transport." Mr. Terrific pointed his index finger at Henry.

"The island tour would have taken you two hours. All you did was drive us two miles for five minutes." Henry looked over at Gavin, who had a smirk on his face. Henry couldn't tell who Gavin was rooting for.

Then Mr. Terrific started with the f-bombs for which he was famous. The litany continued growing louder and louder even as Henry peeled money from his wallet before the neighbors came out and he got thrown out of his place by the condo association.

Mr. Terrific peeled out of the condo entrance while uttering a new string of expletives.

"Don't you have somewhere else I can stay? It's going to be awfully crowded there with the girls and Lisa," Gavin said as Henry hit the code to open the gate to his complex on Gifft Hill.

"No, we're full. And so are the Westin and Caneel Bay, mostly because of the wedding. We're lucky to have Bella Vista for the rest of the family. Besides, won't your family want you with them during such a difficult time? Elena's death has to be a shock for everyone." Henry led Gavin up a slight hill to his unit, where the Ten Villa van awaited them. He hadn't liked Gavin from the first time he met him, when Gavin arrived by helicopter two days before at

Villa Nirvana. Seeing the bruises on Lisa's arms this morning didn't improve Henry's opinion of him.

"Our bags are in the rear," Gavin had told him, ignoring Henry's "Welcome to St. John" greeting. Gavin had gotten off the helicopter without bothering to assist Lisa or his three little girls.

"They'll be fine. The kids barely knew her. Lisa thought she was cold. My mother only met her once. I'm the only one who really knew Elena."

Henry let Gavin into the van, starting the ignition and getting the air conditioning going. The late afternoon sun was relentless, and Gavin was definitely the kind of guy who didn't like to sweat.

"So how well did you know Elena? Did you work with her at the company?"

"I'm the one who hired her. I knew she had what the company needed the moment I met her," Gavin said. Henry was surprised to detect a note of sadness in his voice, although Gavin was probably mourning not Elena but her value to the business.

"Where did you find her?"

"We met at a business conference about exploring borders for companies looking to expand. She had some great ideas. Actually, in many ways, they were quite simple, so much so that they were easy to overlook," Gavin said, as if off in another world. The incongruity between Gavin's callous initial reaction to Elena's death and now his near reverence for her business acumen confused Henry. The guy was odd, at best.

"So how is it your mother came to St. John if she wasn't invited to the wedding?" Henry asked, knowing it was a question Gavin probably wouldn't like, but not really caring much about what he thought at this point.

Gavin surprised him by chuckling.

"One thing I do know, Henry, is this—I have no idea why my mother does anything."

They pulled into the Westin complex, stopping at the gatehouse to find out where Anneka's unit was. Henry stopped at the curb outside of the condo and got out of the van to properly dispose of his human cargo. Gavin was about his age, Henry figured, but they had absolutely nothing in common, and he had no desire to spend more than another second with the man.

"There you go, Gavin. We'll be in touch about what happens next and when you can get your stuff out of Nirvana," Henry said, opening Gavin's door.

Gavin stepped out and reached over the door to pluck a piece of paper from under the van's windshield wiper.

"Looks like you got yourself a ticket somewhere, Henry," Gavin said, giving him a smug smile and handing him a scrap of yellow paper.

Henry stepped back into the van, wondering what he'd done to earn the ticket, especially one he hadn't noticed. He and Sabrina had been careful not to get tickets because they were very expensive on island and almost impossible to appeal in Superior Court, but they had gotten a few unavoidable ones that cost them about seventy-five dollars each. This one didn't look anything like the others he'd gotten. Henry unfolded the ticket to see it wasn't a ticket at all.

On island. Staying at the front cottage at Gibney Beach Villas while I look for long-term housing. Would love some company. Have so much to tell you. Love, David

Chapter Fourteen

Sabrina was looking at the mountainous trays of food scattered across the blue-and-white Scandinavian tiled kitchen counters, wondering what the hell she was going to do with them, when she heard the sound of the van. A little fuzzy from a couple of vodkas, she could sure use some help from Henry, although the sounds of Sean sobbing had pretty much sobered her up.

"Holy crap, what are we supposed to do with all this food?" Henry asked, flinging the two lost-and-found bags onto the floor.

"I was hoping you would know."

"You're the one who grew up in a diner. But I suppose we can figure it out. How's it going here?" Henry asked.

Sabrina filled him in, explaining that Sean had a total meltdown at sunset and that he and the rest of the family were resting until she let them know dinner was ready.

"How did it go with Gavin?" Sabrina asked.

"All right. The guy's not my favorite Keating, shall we say. He didn't seem overly upset about Elena's murder, but got kind of maudlin when he talked about her and the business. Weird," Henry said, lifting covers off of dishes to see what had been delivered. "I think he's been roughing up Lisa. I saw bruises on her arms this morning."

"Oh, that's not good." Sabrina thought there was already enough drama in the Keating family without adding domestic violence to the mix.

"I say we just serve half the food and put the rest in the refrigerator for another meal. Who knows how long the police will keep Villa Nirvana off limits."

"That won't work. Some of this stuff won't keep well, but at least we don't have to worry about reheating anything. I guess Elena's insistence on a cold menu ended up being a good idea after all." Sabrina remembered reviewing the menu with her and Sean at a meeting with Zeus's chef, Carlos Holmes. Chef Holmes had urged Elena to include at least one hot item, but Elena resisted.

"It will be warm at sunset," Elena had proclaimed. "An elegant, cold meal will be perfect, and we won't have to worry about timing things around food." A proud Sean had beamed at her brilliance while Sabrina and Carlos had demurred.

Feta and watermelon salad. Beef carpaccio. Shrimp cocktail with avocado and grapefruit. Lobster tails with mango puree. Artisan rolls. Island-churned butter. Two cases of chilled Veuve Clicquot. It had turned out to be the perfect menu.

"Shall we serve them out by the pool or inside?" Henry asked, beginning to pull plates out of the kitchen cabinets.

"I'd say inside. Then we don't need to worry about no-see-ums." Sabrina often marveled how insects so tiny that they were almost invisible could cause vacationers such misery, arriving at dusk just in time for happy hour. By the next morning, people were itching bites that were ten times the size of the bug that got them.

"Bad enough we had the skinny-dippers here. Gave a little comic relief before it got really heavy," she added. "I just hope they don't come back. The Keatings need privacy. Sean is a mess. Everyone seems to be avoiding the suggestion that Elena may have been murdered. Why would someone kill her?"

"Other than because she refused to sign the prenup? I have no idea, except people didn't seem to warm to her," Henry said.

They set the table in the dining area overlooking the other tropical garden that bordered the front walkway. Moonlight had begun to filter through the trees and shrubs while a gentle breeze rustled through the leaves. Sabrina couldn't help but think that it was a perfect Caribbean evening for a wedding.

Henry knocked on everyone's doors, except Sean's, to let them know dinner was being served.

Heather was the first to enter the kitchen.

"Would either of you know where I might find some aspirin? I never drink in the afternoon and now I remember why." Heather rubbed her temples, groaning.

"Of course, sweetie. I have some in my backpa—oops, I don't have my backpack. It's at Nirvana. Maybe there's some left in one of the medicine cabinets," Henry said as Kate and Jack entered the kitchen.

"I'd love to get out of these clothes. Any idea when we can get some of our stuff from the villa?" Jack asked. Sabrina looked at him, dressed in a now-wrinkled silk shirt and linen pants, guessing this wasn't a standard outfit for a guy in construction.

Henry and Sabrina dragged the two bags of lost and found out into the great room, where they found Paul sitting in a chair looking as if he'd just had a cool shower and put fresh clothes on. They explained that everything in the bags was clean.

"Oh, look. Fabulous!" Heather said, grabbing a shapeless, gaudy, loose-fitting sleeveless dress in an orange-and-green blossom print. The style wasn't very different from the green-and-blue polka-dotted dress Heather was already wearing, except hers had two front pockets, which made it seem even more matronly.

Jack found a pair of Sloop Jones swim trunks, which were hand painted in a wild pattern of red, yellow, and green.

"Way to go, Jack. I don't know how those got by me. Sloop's a local artist and hand paints all his stuff. You just scored," Henry said.

Sabrina winced, catching Paul shaking his head at Henry's familiarity, but Jack just grinned as he reached in trying to find a T-shirt.

Kate found a skirt and tank top.

Henry handed out the toothbrushes and toothpaste that Ten Villas kept stocked. Paul accepted a fresh Izod shirt from Sabrina. It was beginning to feel a little like a party on Gilligan's Island.

Sabrina suggested they all sit so she and Henry could serve them dinner. This time Paul surprised her.

"You and Henry have been working all day, first thinking you were throwing a wedding and then helping us after . . . after, well, you know. Please join us," he said, taking a place at the head of the table, while Jack moved toward the opposite seat, like two chairmen of the board commencing a meeting.

"There's cold champagne I could open, unless you think it inappropriate given the circumstances," Sabrina said, hating how awkward she sounded. But how the hell was she supposed to know if it was bad taste or simply an act of kindness to offer champagne after someone was murdered? Really, she had read all the etiquette books ranging from Miss Manners to Emily Post in an effort to compensate for her own lack of experience, but none of them had prepared her for this. She supposed she had the breeding, given the substantial amount of wealth on her mother's side of the family, but without someone to model manners and social grace, Sabrina had to educate herself on social skills.

"Yes, let's open the champagne and eat and gather our strength for what lies ahead," Kate said, taking a seat next to her husband.

Henry had inserted place settings for them. He sat next to Heather, while Sabrina sat next to Paul on one side with an empty chair reserved for Sean on the other, in case he woke up and decided to join them.

Henry began passing the serving dishes. The conversation dwindled as they ate their way through the wedding menu. Sabrina was impressed by how tasty the combination of salads and cold foods were, silently admiring Elena for being right in all her choices. She felt a little guilty for enjoying a meal that should have been part of the celebration of a marriage, not comfort after a death. But Kate was right. They had all been through an ordeal and needed to fortify themselves. And it wasn't like they were eating the wedding cake, which sat on a shelf in the middle of the refrigerator at Villa Nirvana. Would the police appreciate the elegance of Elena's wedding menu?

She heard the sound of a car engine, then saw lights shining into the garden from the driveway. Who would be coming to Bella Vista at this hour?

Henry rose from the table, leaving the dining room and walking toward the front door as Sabrina heard the loud knocks. After some low murmuring, Henry entered the dining room, followed by Detective Hodge and Sergeant Detree.

"I've come to ask several important questions. First, where are the other two Mr. Keatings? The brothers?"

Sabrina explained where Gavin was staying and that Sean was finally sleeping and should not be disturbed if at all possible.

"Well, if you can answer my questions, we can leave him be," Hodge said, sounding more stern than kind.

"Go ahead and ask," Paul said, leaning forward and staring directly at Hodge with an "I've had enough for one day" face.

Hodge opened the flap to an eight-by-eleven-inch envelope he had tucked under his arm and pulled out a piece of paper wrapped in what Sabrina affectionately called "document raincoats," otherwise known as "sheet protectors." Although she had grown up on the South Shore below Boston on a peninsula that seemed to fluctuate between cold dampness and hot humidity, she had never experienced moisture in the air like she had in the Virgin Islands. Everything got moldy. Shoes, bra straps, sheets, and even paper. Paper became limp and discolored in no time.

Detective Hodge held up the document but didn't remove it from the sheet protector. Sabrina realized he was probably more concerned about fingerprints than moisture if this was evidence in the case. She strained to see what the document was, but Hodge seemed to be teasing them by not bringing it closer.

"There are two signatures on this document. One is above a line with 'Elena Consuela Soto Rodriguez' typed below. The other is a signature above a line typed 'Witness.' I need to know if anyone can confirm that the signature is actually that of Elena Consuela Soto Rodriguez. Of course, we'll have forensics confirm it, but for now if you reasonably believe it is her signature, please indicate so," Hodge said, sounding very formal.

"Secondly, if you can identify the second signature above the word, 'Witness,' it would be most helpful. As you will see, it is not discernible unless you are already familiar with it. I cannot let you touch it, but Sergeant Detree will walk around the table to show it to each of you," Hodge continued.

Sabrina watched as Hodge handed the document in its plastic shrine over to Lucy Detree as if she were his handmaiden. She wanted to kick him in the shins and tell him to walk the damn document around the table himself if it was so important.

"I think it's Elena's signature, if I remember it correctly. No idea about the scrawl below," Jack said.

Heather shook her head when Detree put the paper under her nose.

"I wouldn't know Elena's signature. I don't think I've ever seen it. And whoever signed below should have been a doctor with that penmanship," she said.

Paul gestured for Detree to bring the document closer to him, which she did, but only after looking toward Hodge for approval. Sabrina strained to see what was on the paper. She could only see two lines with handwriting above them. It looked like the signature page to a legal document to her.

"That's Elena's signature as best I can tell," he said. He sat back and then leaned forward toward the document a second time.

"But that other one, that really looks more like scribbling to me. I'm afraid I can't help you with that one." Paul took his cloth napkin, dabbing at beads of sweat above his mouth.

"Do either of you know Ms. Rodriguez's signature?" Detree asked Henry and Sabrina, almost as an oversight before she approached Kate.

"No, I wouldn't remember it if I did," Sabrina said. People sent her signed rental agreements all the time. She barely paid attention to them. She and Henry were looking into switching their rental agreement forms so they could be "signed" online.

"Ditto," Henry said.

"How about you, Mrs. Keating? Is that Elena's signature?" Hodge pressed.

"I don't think I've ever seen anything signed personally by Elena, Detective. She sent her thank you notes for her bridal shower gifts by e-mail. She was more inclined to text message us," Kate said.

"How about the second one, ma'am?" Detree pressed.

"Well, what do you know? I know that signature as well as my own. I've read the document it was on count-less times over the years."

"You do?" Hodge jumped in, clearly excited by Kate's revelation.

"How so, dear?" Jack asked.

"It's Anneka's signature, Jack. The one she finally used to autograph the divorce agreement we fought so hard to have her sign."

Chapter Fifteen

Encouraged by the identification of both signatures, Detective Hodge and Sergeant Detree left as quickly as they had arrived. When pressed by Henry about when they might be able to retrieve some of the Keatings' personal belongings, Hodge was noncommittal.

"Crime doesn't conform to a timeline, Mr. Whitman," Hodge said as Henry shut the door behind them.

Sabrina suggested that everyone change into the outfits they had taken from lost and found and give her their own outfits to have laundered. Only Paul and Sean had had their cell phones with them when the police had steered them away from the beach after Elena's body had been recovered. Henry left Paul a spare charger so they could recharge their phones and stay in touch.

With Sean still sleeping, Sabrina and Henry said goodnight to the remainder of the group, who they left speculating over whether the signatures they had been asked to identify had been on the last page of the prenup.

"Dear God, will this day ever end?" Sabrina said as she got into the passenger seat of the van.

"Not yet. Neil wants us to come to Bar None to talk through some of what's happened," Henry said.

"What has happened, Henry?" Sabrina asked.

"A major debacle that is all on me, that's what's happened," Henry said without hesitation.

"Oh come on, now. You can't take the blame for Elena getting killed."

"No, but I set the stage for Ten Villas to be part of this train wreck. I was so sure it would be good for us. Talk about blind ambition." Sabrina noticed how he slowed the van as they drove along the curve on Centerline Road where Larry had died. Was it just last night?

"Then there's this," Henry said, handing Sabrina a crumpled piece of paper. She clicked the flashlight app on her phone and read the message from David.

"When did you get this?"

"When I dropped Gavin off at the Westin, he noticed it under the windshield. Jerk."

"Who? David or Gavin?" Sabrina asked.

"Both." Henry laughed.

"Why didn't David just call or text you? Why so mysterious?"

"I blocked his number after he called a couple of months ago when he heard about the murder at Villa Mascarpone. He was so 'concerned' about me, but not concerned enough to leave his wife," Henry said as they entered the near empty streets of Cruz Bay.

"What are you going to do?" Sabrina asked, thinking David's timing couldn't have been worse if he was hoping to rekindle his relationship with Henry. She could see how guilty Henry was feeling about insisting they take on Villa Nirvana. He probably wouldn't be receptive to taking new risks in an old relationship that had almost taken him down.

David's betrayal of Henry somehow seemed worse than Ben's infidelity to Sabrina. Ben was just a pig taking another woman to bed, albeit their bed. But David had lied when asked by the airlines if he was being sexually harassed by Henry, or at least he hadn't been firm in denying such. Henry took the fall for "inappropriate and unprofessional behavior toward his superior," that being his pilot, David. David, who had been his lover for more than a year and who had romped and played with him while on layovers throughout the Caribbean, was all of a sudden concerned about hurting his wife, and, more importantly, losing his big fat airline pension. Henry had gotten away with his pension and a settlement from a discrimination claim he lodged against the airlines for sexual harassment by his superior. Allied Air had settled in exchange for a pledge of confidentiality. Excoriated by the experience, Henry gladly pledged his silence.

David had repented, calling and writing to Henry many times, Sabrina knew. Henry never accepted David's apologies. "None of it means anything if he's still with his wife," he told Sabrina. She couldn't disagree, but her heart broke for him each time the wound was reopened.

"Will you go see him?" Sabrina asked as they pulled into an empty parking space near Bar None, the availability of which was a sign of just how late it was.

"I don't know," Henry said grimly.

A bartender Sabrina didn't recognize was wiping down the bar where a couple of late stragglers were sitting, nursing their drinks. Before she could ask for Neil, he came up behind her, placing his hand at the base of her spine.

"Hey Salty, Henry. What can I get you? You guys have had quite the day." Neil motioned for Mark to come take orders after introducing him to Henry and Sabrina.

Sabrina opted for a lemon drop, having suffered through almost an entire day without a single lemon. Henry ordered a double Johnny Walker Blue on the rocks, a sign that he was channeling his very serious father, Sabrina knew from experience.

They took their drinks into a corner booth that had been converted into an office of sorts for Neil, who dropped rattan shades for privacy.

"Are you guys hungry? I can have Mark throw on a couple of burgers," Neil offered.

"God no, we just ingested the entire wedding feast up at Bella Vista," Henry said, taking a sip of his scotch.

"How's it going up there? Is Sean beginning to grasp what's happened?"

"Yes. At sunset, when he should have been getting married, he lost it. I think it finally hit him that Elena was gone forever," Sabrina said.

"Tough. Cassie hit that point last night at the clinic when they finally cleaned Larry up enough to let her see him to say good-bye," Neil said.

Sabrina could see how difficult that must have been for Neil, who seemed to cope with life's challenges by coming up with ways to beat them. Larry and Elena's deaths were challenges that no one could beat.

"We did learn some information that might be useful," Sabrina said, wanting to inject an iota of optimism into the conversation.

"Good, because I learned some information that I think you ought to be concerned about," Neil said.

Henry looked up. Sabrina sensed his concern, which heightened her own.

"What's that?" Henry asked.

"When I got tossed from Nirvana by that asshole Hodge, I decided to give Lee a call and find out what's with Hodge," Neil said.

Lee was Leon Janquar, the police detective Sabrina had come to cordial terms with and had hoped would be dispatched to Villa Nirvana when she called. Neil and Lee enjoyed a mutual respect and camaraderie.

"And?" Sabrina asked, knowing what was coming wasn't good.

"This is strictly on the QT. Lee stuck out his neck sharing this with me. It seems Detective Hodge is a pretty ambitious guy and is taking advantage of Lee being out for a month for knee surgery. Hodge has been under fire after an investigation into police misconduct in the Virgin Islands. It seems the men under Hodge have a propensity for violence," Neil said, taking a moment to holler over to Mark to bring him a Guinness.

"He's pretty nasty, even to Lucy Detree," Henry noted. Sabrina was grateful she wasn't the only one who'd witnessed how Hodge treated Lucy earlier in the evening. After her experience in Nantucket when the police had bullied her before she had hired an attorney, Sabrina could never tell if she was overreacting to cops. But she had seen a public service announcement on local television recently that gave detailed instructions about how to file a complaint against a Virgin Island police officer for misconduct, so she knew the department was in trouble.

Neil took a swig out of the bottle of Guinness, his favorite, which Sabrina kept stocked in her refrigerator for their relaxing nights on her porch.

"Well, apparently he has a hair across his ass about Ten Villas and especially you, Salty. He didn't like it that you managed to turn the murder out at Villa Mascarpone around and got a certificate of heroism from the department. And he thinks you got away with murder on Nantucket."

Sabrina treasured her certificate, which had been personally given to her by Lee Janquar. She bit back an unladylike comment and kept listening while Neil continued with the bad news.

"There's no way he can pin Elena's death on Sabrina," Henry said with conviction.

"No, that's not his angle. He's going to go after your Ten Villa's real estate broker's license. He's saying you don't know how to protect the public and that you place them in jeopardy by using poor judgment. Two murders at your villas in three months is his proof. He's also going to enlist the press in his attack, including that barracuda Faith Chase," Neil said.

"That is just so unfair!" Sabrina realized as she said it how ridiculous that sounded. When had anything in recent years been anything but unfair?

"We better set this story straight quickly then," Henry said.

"Yes, the sooner the better. You need to show that Elena's death has nothing to do with the villa's management and everything to do with whoever was motivated to kill her and why," Neil agreed. "The story starts with Elena. What do we know about her?"

Sabrina shared with Henry and Neil what she'd learned about Elena's background, and Henry reported on his ride with Gavin.

"Good work, Salty. I'll make a couple of calls about Elena in the morning. I know a couple of lawyers up in the Boston area who should be able to help with the Harvard and Babson connections," Neil said.

"Maybe someone should check out her history in San Juan at the *caserio*. I could try to go over tomorrow."

"Not without playing into Hodge's hand, Henry. You were told not to go off island, remember?" Neil asked. "I could go, but I'd need to fly. I've got two bartenders out right now. A boat would take too long. I'd wait until Monday to be sure government offices were open," Neil said.

"You won't get in trouble for doing this, Neil?" Sabrina asked. She remembered Hodge's foreboding words about practicing law without a license.

"Hell no, Salty. I've got every right to go to San Juan and look information up. But thanks for watching my back. This would be a lot easier if Larry were still around. We could hop over in his seaplane and be back in a couple of hours," Neil sighed, taking the last draw of his beer.

Sabrina toyed with the lemon slice now sitting at the bottom of her empty glass.

"Would Cassie be willing to rent the seaplane?" she asked, looking over at Henry.

"Sure, but who's going to fly it? No one on the island that I know has a pilot's license," Neil said.

"Unfortunately, someone I know does." Henry raised his glass in a mock toast.

Chapter Sixteen

Sabrina woke early the next morning without an alarm. She had so much to do, so she leapt out of bed and began making a list. She loved lists. They made her feel as if she had some control over her life. And when she crossed off items, she knew she was in charge, or at least felt accomplished.

Before she went to bed, she had remembered her promise to get the fresh laundry over to the Keatings first thing in the morning. Exhausted, she hadn't worried too much about special-care instructions and had dumped the contents of the black plastic bag into the washing machine with a small amount of detergent because the water on island came from cisterns that collected rain water, which was softer. Everything got washed on cold. Island living was pretty simple.

The first item on her list was to "put clothes in dryer." Next, "call Cynthia at St. John Car Rental to let her know her jeeps are in police custody and might not be returned on time." Third, she needed to call her friend Lyla Banks to make sure Girlfriend, who was staying with the Banks while Sabrina worked the Keating wedding, was okay. She added an item to remind her to pick up Henry for their mission to speak to David.

After making a mug of French roast coffee, Sabrina went over to the washing machine, which was located in a small alcove outside of her kitchen. She opened the lid to the machine and began lifting items out and loading them into the dryer.

She smiled as she took Jack's linen pants out of the washer, thinking he looked pretty happy in that Sloop Jones bathing suit and might not want to climb back into hot, scratchy linen. Kate's painting clothes went in next, followed by Paul's shirt. Sabrina reached to grab Heather's blue-and-green dress, something Ruth, the woman who had raised her, would have called a "muumuu," when she felt something in the pocket. She grasped the object and was surprised to find herself holding a platinum necklace with three large, princess-cut stones that looked to be diamonds.

Sabrina held the necklace up, now seeing that one side of the flat chain was shorter than the other and had been broken. The stones were large, at least a carat each judging from what Sabrina has seen in engagement rings. She had never had a diamond because Ben had thought them silly. Of course he had. He'd already bought two of them, one for each of her predecessors.

"Why you could buy a boat or a car for that kind of money," he'd told her, so she'd settled for a Claddagh wedding band, cliché even for Irish American Boston, with the hands, heart, and crown symbolizing friendship, love, and loyalty. Oh what a crock.

Sabrina had known a few women who had three-diamond necklaces, each stone symbolizing one of her children. She knew from ads in magazines they were often touted as a way to memorialize, "the past, present, and future" of a relationship.

Whatever the symbolism was, Sabrina knew she was looking at a stunning and very expensive piece of jewelry. She hadn't seen Heather wearing the necklace, which she surely would have noticed. It definitely wasn't something you would wear with a muumuu. She couldn't imagine why Heather was carrying it in her pocket, other than the chain was broken and couldn't be worn. Sabrina placed the pendant in a small plastic sandwich bag, zipped up the seal, and tucked it in her own pocket. Making a mental note to ask Heather about the necklace later, she finished placing the laundry in the dryer and moved down her list.

Cynthia was sorry to hear that the wedding had turned into a tragedy and would wait to hear about when the jeeps would be returned. Sabrina had rented them for a week in case the family decided to extend their trip and was confident she would have them back at St. John Car Rental by the end of the rental agreement.

Lyla Banks answered her phone on the first ring.

"Girlfriend is having a nice visit. She and Evan are out for a little walk. But how are you, dear? We've heard the news about the poor bride accidentally drowning before the wedding. You and Henry must be a wreck."

Sabrina assured Lyla that she and Henry were coping as best they could, asking if Girlfriend could hang out with them a little longer. She didn't bother correcting Lyla's version about how Elena drowned. Everyone on island would know the facts soon enough.

"She can stay as long as you need. Honestly, she is so good with Evan, I might consider getting a dog for him. He seems more relaxed, and the Alzheimer's symptoms aren't as apparent. Taking care of the dog makes him work at remembering," Lyla said.

After hanging up with Lyla, Sabrina folded the now-dry laundry, placing it in a basket. Within fifteen minutes, her jeep was climbing up Bordeaux Mountain for the second time in less than ten hours. She hoped the Keatings had been able to sleep. Henry should be there already, since he was on breakfast duty.

The smell of bacon wafting through the open windows brought Sabrina right back to Allerton, where she had grown up next to a diner and where bacon was considered medicinal. Bacon could make anything better. Bacon and fried egg sandwiches. Bacon baked on top of meatloaf. BLT's on white bread with Hellman's mayonnaise. She hoped bacon was doing its magic this morning.

She found all of them sitting back at the dining room table where she had left them the night before. They all looked comical in their lost-and-found outfits, other than Sean. He was still in the outfit he had put on twenty-four hours earlier when he'd set out on his doomed mission to find Elena and tell her he didn't care about the prenup.

Henry was removing empty plates where only traces of egg yolk remained. He cooked a great breakfast, Sabrina knew firsthand, although he would always say hers were better.

She set the basket with clean laundry over on a small buffet table.

"I'll just leave these here for you in case you want to change back into your things."

"Hell no, I want to go buy more of what I'm wearing." Jack pointed to his Sloop Jones outfit.

"I'm not sure about that, but if we're not going to get our own personal belongings soon, then I would like to go shopping for a few items," Paul looked uncomfortable in wrinkled clothes. Sabrina imagined he was the kind of man who wore jeans that had been ironed and had a crease—that is, if he wore jeans.

"I'm fine in my painting clothes, but would love to get my hands on a sketching pad," Kate said.

Heather sat silent, looking over at Sean who had his forehead in his hands.

"You're wondering how we can be going on and on, like this is just another day, aren't you?" she said to him.

Sean nodded without looking up.

"I'm sorry, dear. I don't mean to be insensitive." Kate reached across the table to take his hand.

"There are things we need to consider. I know Gavin was premature and inconsiderate yesterday when he dove right into business, but practically speaking we need to talk about how to handle this from our company's perspective. This could be disastrous for Keating Construction just as we're beginning our expansion into villa construction. I think we ought to get Gavin over here and have a board meeting," Paul said.

"A board meeting? Are you frigging kidding me?" Sean asked, rising from the table and turning around to leave the room just as Neil Perry entered. Neil was holding a box of baked goods from the island bakery, Baked in the Sun.

"Hold on a minute, Sean," Neil said, putting the box on the table. "I can appreciate you're not up for a board meeting, but I'm here trying to help sort the Elena situation out for you. We just have to be a little discreet here, like I'm just bringing you a few island pastries and muffins as a measure of kindness. What we talk about is just a civilized conversation between a guy and his former lawyer after a tragic event. Just a little man-talk. Nothing legal, of course."

Sabrina had half-expected something like this. She knew Neil liked to be in charge, that him taking a backseat in the investigation wouldn't last.

"Well, you guys have your chat. I'm changing back into my clean painting clothes." Kate walked over and started handing the others their items from the laundry basket. In short time, only Henry, Sabrina, and Neil remained in the dining room with Sean.

"Listen, buddy. I know this has been hell for you, but you want to know who did this, don't you?" Neil asked Sean, sitting down and gesturing for Sean to take the chair next to him.

"Of course," Sean said, taking the chair.

"Even if some stuff comes out that you don't necessarily like?" Neil asked.

"What do you mean?" Sean asked. Sabrina wasn't sure where Neil was going, but she found it impossible not to feel sorry for Sean.

"Well, Elena may have had a few secrets. Most of us do. I'll bet you didn't share with her every little tidbit that was in my files about you," Neil said.

"Of course not," Sean almost smiled.

Sabrina and Henry listened to the conversation silently, turning their heads from Sean to Neil as if at a tennis match.

"It turns out that Elena didn't graduate from Babson or Harvard, at least not under the name Elena Consuela Soto Rodriguez. Maybe you got the schools confused. Maybe she used a different name in the states. Perhaps she fudged her credentials a bit. Lots of people do. But it doesn't check out."

"But I saw the diplomas on her office wall. Gavin checked her references and resume when he hired her," Sean said.

"It gets confusing when people use two last names, which is common in the Hispanic community. Maybe they were reversed or misspelled. Would it help to check the marriage license? Henry, can you get your hands on it so we can see if there's a spelling error?" Sabrina asked.

"Uh, not easily. I was nervous I would forget where I had put it. I mean, it was the first wedding I was performing and I didn't want anything to go wrong, so I put it someplace where I knew I wouldn't be able to forget it." Henry looked sheepish. Sabrina was afraid of what was coming next. Sometimes Henry's sense of logic seemed unique to him. He would frequently tuck objects, like keys, in odd places like microwaves as reminders that he needed to go to a certain place. Sabrina might find the extra flatware in the wine cellar and have to ask Henry why it was there. "So we'll remember it's time to replace the batteries in the smoke detectors, of course," Henry would say, as if Sabrina was silly not to already know.

"Henry?" Sabrina pressed.

"I put it in an envelope and then stuck it in a sheet protector and placed it under the wedding cake in the refrigerator. I knew I would remember it that way," Henry said.

Sabrina stifled the urge to groan.

"Okay, so we'll have to wait to verify the spelling of the names and then I'll double check the school records.

But Sean, you can see why it's necessary to know as much as we can about Elena. Right now the cops are collecting evidence that they hope will point them toward the person who killed her. They're going to want to find a person who had a motive and doesn't have an alibi. You could be their best candidate. You've got to understand. Police investigations don't work the same way here as they do in the States."

Sean's tanned face drained to a pasty gray.

"But it sounds like she did sign the prenup. Those detectives were here last night asking if anyone could identify the signatures on a document. It had to be the prenup. Why would any of us want to kill Elena if she had signed it?" Sean asked.

"Did any of your family know she signed it?" Neil asked.

"No, of course not. They would have been thrilled that the whole issue was resolved and the wedding could go forward. The only one who would have known for sure was the witness. Gavin's mother."

Chapter Seventeen

Sabrina and Henry left Neil with Sean, who was pulling up a copy of the draft of the prenup he had on his phone so Neil could review it. She hoped Detective Hodge didn't make another surprise visit to Bella Vista, but she couldn't save Neil from himself any more than he could do the same for her, much as he tried.

Henry hadn't been wild about approaching David to fly Neil to San Juan the following morning. But he eventually accepted that unless Elena's murder was solved, Ten Villas would continue to be under scrutiny and possibly subject to a trumped-up charge of negligence. Without a real estate broker's license, Ten Villas was out of business.

"You don't think you should call him first?" Sabrina asked. She'd offered to drive to Gibney Beach, knowing Henry was a wreck. She couldn't blame him. He hadn't seen David for a long time. Now he was forced to meet him face-to-face and ask for a favor at the same time.

"No. I want him to be as uncomfortable as I am," Henry said. "And that's pretty damn uncomfortable."

"I'm sorry," Sabrina didn't know how to comfort him. It was not lost on her that Henry was dressed far less colorfully than usual. Instead of a tropical print shirt or his beloved New England madras shorts, he was wearing khaki shorts and a plain white T-shirt.

"It's not your fault. Remember, I'm the idiot who forced Villa Nirvana on you."

"It seems like such a silly name now for the villa. Nirvana. 'Stillness, after the extinction of desire.' Hardly," Sabrina said, trying to distract Henry from his guilt.

"What? Oh, you're talking Nirvana as in Buddhism. That's not what it's named after."

"I thought it was supposed to be a new age spiritual retreat with a business twist. That's what Elena told me when we met with the chef."

"Hell, no. Sean told me he named it after Kurt Cobain's band," Henry said.

That sounded to Sabrina more like the Sean that Neil had told Sabrina he'd represented in LA—fun-loving, ambitious, a little reckless, and a bit of a womanizer. It seemed to Sabrina that Elena had almost cast a spell over Sean, transforming or perhaps reforming him into a serious, although still ambitious, paragon of virtue. *How had she done that?* Sabrina wondered. How can one human being influence another so profoundly? She just couldn't get a handle on Elena. And she'd never been able to get under the skin of another human being like that. At least, not that she knew of.

They arrived at the imposing black wrought-iron gates, which were closed but not locked. The gates said "Oppenheimer Beach," but many people referred to it as Gibney. The beach below the steep driveway, which lay beyond the gates, was named for the two families who had settled there. No matter which name you called it, it was Sabrina's favorite bit of coastline, the spot where she and Girlfriend swam to each night from the next beach, Hawksnest.

Early beach goers took the four parking spaces located right outside the gates, but since she and Henry were actually guests of one of the people renting a Gibney villa, they used the private driveway that ran down to the cottages.

They parked to the right of a rental jeep with the name of a St. Thomas car rental company on it. Sabrina and Henry always recommended that their villa guests stick to car rental agencies located on St. John to avoid the need to take the car ferry and also to avoid the complications that could occur if the vehicle needed repairs.

"Jerk. He doesn't even know where to rent a jeep from." Henry slid out of the Ten Villas van.

"Well, how would he if someone didn't tell him?" Sabrina asked. She thought that Henry should maybe go a little easy on David, especially since they were there to ask him for a big favor.

They walked up the driveway past the "Garden Cottage" and the "Orchid House," which separated it from the "Beach Cottage" where David was staying. David had opted for one of the few accommodations on island where you could roll out of bed and land directly on white sand, within a few steps of warm turquoise water. Sabrina had always thought it was the perfect spot for a honeymoon, not that she was ever going to get another one. She and Ben had spent theirs in Detroit during the playoffs one year when the Red Sox had managed to exceed everyone's expectations in Boston and Ben had been covering the game.

Henry stopped in his tracks and pointed toward a chaise on the beach where a man in a Boston Red Sox cap, swim trunks, and sunglasses sat reading a very thick book. They would be approaching David from the rear, surprising him. Sabrina would take her cues from Henry. Even though they were there to ask for help protecting their business, Henry deserved the courtesy of choosing how.

"Good morning, David," Henry called out, reminding Sabrina a little of Robin Williams's titular greeting in *Good Morning, Vietnam.*

David swung his feet quickly off the chaise and stood up, dropping *The Goldfinch* onto the sand. Sabrina bent over to pick it up, grateful for a few seconds of relief when her eyes did not have to bear witness to this awkward moment.

"Henry, and this must be—"

"Sabrina Salter, David. So nice to finally meet you." Sabrina used her best manners, the ones Henry exemplified, as she handed David the book and then her hand, which David shook. She was surprised to see that David was completely bald, which made his deep-green eyes pop. He was taller than she was, making him much taller than Henry, whom she towered over.

"Please, come up on the porch. Can I get you coffee, maybe a beer, or is it too early?" David asked, clearly rattled by their surprise appearance. Sabrina felt a little sorry for him, but then remembered what a prick he'd been to Henry.

"Never too early for a beer on an island, right, Sabrina?" Henry said.

"The breakfast of champions." Sabrina followed Henry as David led them through the white-picket gate and up the stairs to the front porch, gesturing toward chairs for them to sit in.

"I'd love a cold water. I have a pretty gruesome day at work ahead and think I'd better leave alcohol out of it, at least until it's over," Sabrina said.

"I've heard about the death of the bride. It's all over the news." David glanced over at Henry.

"Shit." Sabrina sunk into an Adirondack chair.

"What are they saying?" Henry slumped into the chair next to Sabrina.

"That she drowned the night before her wedding to a big-shot businessman and that they don't know if it's suicide or an accident." David cleared his throat and edged toward the kitchen. "Let me grab those waters."

"Henry, we need to ask David fast if he'll help. Before this gets worse and the media finds out that Elena was actually murdered," Sabrina said quietly, leaning over toward Henry so David wouldn't hear.

"I get it."

David returned with three bottles of water and three glasses.

"You can skip the glasses. We really can't stay long. As much as it's killing me, I'm really here to ask a favor, David." Henry paused, Sabrina assumed, waiting to see how David was reacting to his abrupt revelation.

"Okay, what can I do for you?" David asked evenly, handing them each a bottle of water, then sitting on a stool opposite the Adirondack chairs.

Sabrina decided to jump in at this point, since David seemed willing to listen and Henry had already done the hard part. She quickly summarized what had taken place the day and night before and how they'd come to realize it was impossible to make sense of Elena's murder without knowing more about her history, which involved growing up in San Juan.

"Neil Perry, who used to practice law in California, is willing to go and dig up whatever facts he can from local legal records, but the only way to get to San Juan and back fast is to fly. Of course, you know there's no airport on St. John. The commercial flights out of St. Thomas wouldn't give him enough time in Puerto Rico before having to return to his business here. He would've asked the one guy on St. John who has his own seaplane to fly him over, but he was killed in a car accident the same night

Elena died. No connection, just an unfortunate coincidence, but what we're left with is—" Sabrina stopped to catch her breath, realizing just how ridiculous and pitiful at the same time the whole story was sounding. Henry must have sensed this and came to her rescue.

"What we're left with, David, is a seaplane without a pilot. And what Sabrina is so kindly omitting from the story is that on top of all of everything else, this is all my fault. I was bullheaded about adding this over-the-top villa to our cadre of rental homes, refusing to listen to the very good reasons she was against it. Now the local police want to use Elena's murder at one of our villas, after another death a few months ago also connected to our business, as mounting evidence that we are incapable, negligent at protecting the public, and should not have a real estate license allowing us to rent to the public. They want to shut us down."

Sabrina was shocked that Henry had been willing to fall on his sword for her in front of David, an act that must feel humiliating. It was far greater than any apology he might ever offer her. She watched as Henry and David locked eyes with one another without exchanging words.

"You want me to fly Neil Perry to San Juan. When?" David asked, turning to Sabrina.

"First thing tomorrow. Will you do it?"

"Of course. I will do whatever it takes. Whatever it takes," David said, but this time he was talking to Henry.

Chapter Eighteen

Sabrina checked her cell phone for messages once she and Henry were back in the van. Reception was so spotty on island that you had to check frequently if you wanted to be able to respond to things as they came in. Sure enough, there was one from Detective Hodge, which she played for Henry, instructing her to have her guests return to Villa Nirvana at 3:00 when they could pick up some of their possessions and be interviewed. They would not be permitted to stay at the villa until the "public safety issues" had been resolved. It wasn't necessary for the young Keating children to come.

Sabrina fumed. Public safety issues. What BS. They needed to resolve Elena's murder quickly before Hodge used this subterfuge to undermine their entire business. Henry had managed to spin the last murder at one of their villas so that people were actually clamoring to stay there, but a second homicide might be pushing it.

"I appreciate how difficult it must have been for you to ask David for help, Henry. Let me make the next part of your day a little easier. I'll pick up Gavin and Lisa at the Westin. You can take the rest of the clan up at Bella Vista. It's my turn to deal with Gavin," Sabrina said.

"Okay," Henry sighed. Sabrina wasn't sure if he wanted to talk about David or not. She wanted to be a supportive friend but wasn't sure if that meant letting Henry have some time to digest his first meeting with David or encouraging him to talk about it. How did people know these things? Why didn't she have this sense others seemed to take for granted? She plunged in any way.

"'Whatever it takes' is a huge commitment," Sabrina said.

"David's good at words. Let's see him put them into action."

Sabrina drove to Henry's condominium on Gifft Hill and switched to the Ten Villas Jeep Wrangler since she would have only two passengers. She called Lisa Keating's cell phone rather than Gavin's and left a message that she would pick them up shortly. Sabrina had been careful to collect the cell phone numbers of the entire Keating clan before they'd arrived on St. John. With so many people attending an event and staying at various places, the chances of something unplanned happening were high. She just hadn't known it would be a murder.

Lisa answered the door before Sabrina had a chance to knock. She was dressed in a different outfit than Sabrina remembered from the beach just twenty-four hours earlier. The Westin had several high-fashion, pricey boutiques, and Lisa was definitely not dressed in clothes from the lost-and-found bags. Sabrina noted she was wearing a blouse with long sleeves that covered the marks on her arms.

"I saw you coming. Kind of hard to miss that shade of green," Lisa said, smiling.

"A business decision I have lived to regret," Sabrina said, not for the first time wishing she and Henry had not chosen the gecko-green color for their Wrangler, but she laughed with Lisa, whom she noticed was sipping what appeared to be a Bloody Mary.

"Can I offer you one?" Lisa asked.

"I better not. Where's Gavin?" Sabrina asked, looking around the spacious but generically decorated room.

"He's going to meet us there. He had some calls to make and the reception here is lousy, so he drove over to the Park Department, where Anneka said he'd have four bars. He's really worried about how Elena's death will affect the company."

What a pompous prig, Sabrina thought. Gavin was more worried about collateral damage to the business than he was about his family. His half brother's bride is murdered and all he can think about is how it could hurt Keating Construction. She hoped Detective Hodge wouldn't be annoyed with her because Gavin was coming on his own rather than in her care. At this point, Hodge was ready to pile the blame on Ten Villas for just about anything.

"Are the kids with him?" Sabrina asked, realizing how quiet the condo was.

"Are you kidding? No, Gavin wouldn't know what to do with one of the girls, let alone all three. They're with Anneka over at the hotel pool," Lisa said, sipping the last of her drink.

"Do I have time for a refill?"

Ever the good girl, Sabrina was ready to tell her no, that Lisa ought to be sober when she talked to the police because you never know how they're going to interpret your words. Then she realized she wasn't in charge of Lisa and that maybe Lisa had some information that might shed light on the situation.

"Sure. Do you have a bottle of water?"

"Of course. There's no shortage of all things liquid on this island, is there?" Lisa said, pouring more vodka than tomato juice into her glass, then handing Sabrina a grapefruit San Pellegrino.

"That's the truth." Sabrina thought Lisa would probably succumb to the temptations of island living if left on St. John for too long. For so many people, the booze just flowed too easily to resist and before you knew it, you were either on your way back home after blowing all your money or sitting under the pavilion at Hawksnest at an AA meeting trying to sort it all out with others who had the same proclivity.

"Were you and Elena close?" Sabrina asked, sliding onto a stool at an island counter that separated the living room from the kitchen.

"Close? Ha. I don't think Elena was close to anyone, including Sean."

"Why do you say that?" Sabrina asked, hoping she wasn't pushing too hard. She had no way to gauge it if she were, so why not try?

"Elena wasn't the kind of woman you got close to. I mean, I can't imagine going shopping or gossiping with her. She was always planning, thinking. She definitely had a mind for business."

"Not exactly the one who baked cookies or hosted holidays, I gather," Sabrina offered, not feeling like she had a pulse on Elena yet.

"Well, funny you should mention that. She wasn't very domestic, but she was so competitive that it didn't stop her from trying to control the family holidays."

"What do you mean?"

"It will probably sound stupid to you, but growing up in an Italian family, Christmas Eve was huge. The Feast of the Seven Fishes was a family tradition and then we'd all go to Midnight Mass," Lisa said.

"I've heard of it. Where did you grow up?" Sabrina asked, surprised to hear Lisa was of Italian descent. She had assumed Lisa was Scandinavian like her mother-in-law, since they were both blonde, which of course was ridiculous because there are blonde Italians and there are plenty of blondes who are not naturally so.

"Providence, Rhode Island. Federal Hill. You probably never heard of it," Lisa said.

Sabrina shook her head. "Wrong. I'm from Boston. That's where the best restaurants in Providence are."

"Right. So ever since I married Gavin and moved to the West Coast, away from my family, I've hosted a traditional Italian Christmas Eve at our home in Corte Madera. I serve seven fish dishes ranging from traditional *baccala* to lobster bisque, in honor of Kate's Boston roots. The girls help me—well, as much as they can—and it's become our family tradition. Or had, I should say, until Elena butted in," Lisa said.

"How so?"

"She insisted on hosting a traditional Puerto Rican Christmas celebration, which of course is also on Christmas Eve. If we were welcoming her into our family, she was sure we would want to include her ethnic heritage, blah, blah, blah. Jack and Kate didn't know what to say. Sean was so gaga over Elena, it never occurred to him that this might be hurtful to me and the girls. He and Elena weren't even living together. And Gavin, well, he said it all came down to a business decision. Since Elena was now an important part of the business, he told me to get over it, that I knew where my bread was buttered. Christmas Eve was reduced to a professional choice."

"I'm sorry," Sabrina said and meant it. Elena wasn't turning out to be a very nice woman.

"Here's the kicker. Sure, Elena served a traditional Puerto Rican meal at her apartment. We had roasted pig, *pasteles*, *gandules*, and even a fabulous *tembleque*, which is a coconut custard that my girls loved. But Elena didn't cook any of it. She had it prepared by a local Puerto Rican housecleaner and paid for it. She barely touched the food, saying she was more into vegetarian or pescatarian cuisine now. Pescatarian! Tell me, what is more pescatarian than the menu for the Feast of the Seven Fishes?"

"That must have been tough."

"Everything has been tough since Elena landed into the family. She was so divisive. But Kate said she'd tamed Sean, which was long overdue. He had been living a little too wildly and dangerously."

"Are he and Gavin as different as they seem?"

"Oh yeah. Like night and day. Gavin's all business and Sean, well, at least before Elena, was all play," Lisa said, pulling her hair back into an imaginary ponytail.

Sabrina didn't think first. She just asked. It had been bothering her ever since Henry told her about the marks on Lisa's arms.

"Lisa, I don't want to intrude, but Henry saw the marks on your arms yesterday morning. I know it's not really my business, except isn't it everyone's business to be safe and help other women stay safe? What I'm asking is, do you feel safe? Do you need help?"

Lisa flinched and then turned redder than the Bloody Mary she had just finished.

"Look, we've been going through a rough spot. We're just about to celebrate our tenth anniversary, so who wouldn't expect a marriage to have a little hiccup?"

"But do you feel safe?" Sabrina asked, figuring she had already fired all her bullets.

"Everyone was so charged up that night. People screaming at Elena to sign the damn prenup. Elena was hysterical, a first, telling everyone she wouldn't sign the prenup. The wedding be damned. I had had enough of the drama and enough wine that I pulled Gavin to the side and suggested we had better things we could be doing on a warm Caribbean night. The girls were already asleep. He wasn't exactly receptive to my advances, having been part of the hollering faction. But I persisted until he finally grabbed me by the arms and told me if I wanted to go to bed now, I was welcome to, but that it would be alone. He pressed hard enough to leave those marks, but it's really my fault for pressuring him. I decided to sleep in the girls' room and let him cool off. I shouldn't have been so over-bearing." Lisa sounded pretty sober for a woman who'd just downed two strong drinks.

It's really my fault? I pressured him to come make love to me? Was Sabrina hearing this right? She didn't really know what to say next, so she said nothing.

"Look, Sabrina, I know Gavin can be a jerk. Believe me, I probably know better than anyone. But you have to remember that he hasn't always had it easy. Overbearing doesn't begin to describe his mother. She and Jack had the divorce from hell. Then Jack remarries and has another son who displaces Gavin as sole heir. Even Heather diluted Jack's attention. And Kate was such a warm, loving stepmother, she made Anneka look even worse than she is."

"Lisa, you don't have to defend Gavin to me," Sabrina said. What she didn't say is there's no defense for a man abusing his wife.

"Things have been a little better. I know Gavin was about to surprise me with a generous and thoughtful gift for our anniversary. He doesn't know that I found it in his toiletry bag when I was looking for dental floss. I'll act surprised when he finally gives it to me," Lisa said, not seeming to be able to stop herself.

Why do women continue to delude themselves like this? Sabrina wanted to scream. Instead, she decided to pacify Lisa.

"What is it?"

"It's a lovely necklace with three princess-cut diamonds, symbolizing each of our daughters," Lisa said, beaming.

Chapter Nineteen

Henry was grateful for the quiet time during his drive up to Bordeaux Mountain to retrieve the Keating family. He needed to digest what had just happened. Seeing David sitting on the beach at Gibney felt unnaturally natural. The moment should have felt more awkward, but it didn't. Blurting out to David that he'd made a mess out of life by foisting Villa Nirvana on Sabrina and asking for help wasn't how he'd intended to approach the situation. Not much of anything he'd planned lately went accordingly. Maybe he was just too much of a control freak.

He pulled into the shady driveway of Bella Vista, wishing he could just take the day off, go to the beach like everyone who came to visit St. John. Henry had learned early that living on an island didn't mean you got to go to the beach every day. Sometimes you had to work so hard to afford living here, you could go weeks without a day off.

He spotted Heather sitting on a chaise in the orchid garden with a closed book on her lap. That was another thing he missed—time to read.

"Book no good?" he asked.

Heather looked up at him, shaking her head.

"I wouldn't know. I can't see well enough to read without my glasses, but I thought I'd give it a try."

"Oh, I'm sorry. I guess they're back at Villa Nirvana. Well, you'll have them back soon. We can pick up everyone's stuff, but unfortunately they won't let you stay there just yet." Henry was furious Detective Hodge was capitalizing on the situation and using it to discredit Ten Villas.

"Don't be. I like this house much better. Villa Nirvana may be grander, but it's got no heart. This house feels like it's been lived in and loved."

Henry sat down in the chair opposite Heather. He wasn't looking forward to returning to Nirvana, where he knew they were all going to be treated to a whole lot more than just the opportunity for the Keatings to retrieve their property. Henry dreaded being interviewed by the police, even though he hadn't done anything near criminal. He'd just been stupid. Why had he inserted himself in the conflict about the prenup? It really had nothing to do with Ten Villas. Had he been egotistical about performing a "celebrity" wedding of sorts as his first wedding? Or was he drawn to drama? That was something David, and more recently Sabrina, had suggested.

"The Falks have owned this house for decades. Anything they do to it is first rate. Look at the Swedish tiles throughout the house, and that kitchen is to die for." Henry liked that Heather appreciated Bella Vista.

"I really don't think it's a good idea to put us all under one roof right now, especially not at Villa Nirvana," Heather said.

"I get the Villa Nirvana part, but why wouldn't you all want to be together at a time like this?"

"I don't think my family will ever be the same after this, Henry. Not that we were perfect before. There's always been tension between Gavin and Sean, especially when Elena became part of the picture."

"Well, not to be insensitive, but with Elena gone, won't the family situation improve? And why did Elena make Sean and Gavin more at odds? I don't get it." The enigmatic Elena seemed as mysterious in life as in her death.

"She was Sean's fiancée, but she was Gavin's business protégé, although sometimes it really appeared that Elena was in charge. Once Gavin hired her, everything changed. Keating Construction was transformed from a parking garage construction firm to one building luxury villas for elite international businesses. With Jack and Paul ready to retire in three years, Gavin and Elena, and eventually Sean once he became smitten with Elena, persuaded them the company needed to take a new direction if it was to grow," Heather said, placing the book on the table next to her. Henry could see she had picked up Herman

Wouk's *Don't Stop the Carnival*, a classic spoof about chasing dreams of living in the Caribbean.

"Was Sean opposed to building villas at first?" Henry asked.

"Yes, that is until Elena cast her spell over him and turned him into a company man. Don't get me wrong, Sean was a bit wild and could have used a little taming, but this was like he'd found religion. He's furious at Gavin for insisting Elena sign the prenup. He's also upset with Jack and Paul for pushing it, but Gavin was the driving force," Heather said.

"I can see how that could splinter a family, but it's not like Elena was driven to suicide because of the prenup. And I could see Sean being angry enough to kill Gavin. But it's not like Gavin killed her," Henry said, thinking how his life as an only child had been a little lonely, but much less complicated.

"We don't know that, do we?" Heather said with a lift of her eyebrow.

Chapter Twenty

Sabrina looked over at Lisa, who was dozing in the passenger seat of the jeep after her Bloody Mary lunch, which was a relief. It gave her time before she arrived at Villa Nirvana to consider what she should do next. What was she supposed to do with the diamond necklace sitting in her tote bag in the backseat? She'd meant to return it to Heather earlier this morning when she brought the clean laundry to the Keatings, but then Sean had had another freak-out and she had gotten distracted. What if someone thought she stole it? That was all Detective Hodge would need to banish her from St. John.

She didn't understand how or why Heather had the diamond necklace Gavin was giving to Lisa for their anniversary. And how had it gotten broken? Had Gavin broken it and asked Heather to get it fixed before he gave it to Lisa? Should she just hand it over to Detective Hodge, inform him how she came into possession of it, and let him figure it out? No, that would be crazy, Sabrina decided. When did telling the truth become so hard? But she knew the answer to that question. It all came back to the moment when she pulled the trigger and shot Ben. Nothing in her life, not even telling the truth, had ever been simple after she fired the gun that night.

Sabrina drove down the steep hill known as Jacob's Ladder into Cruz Bay. Never a fan of heights, it had terrified her when she first arrived in St. John, but she had gotten used to it and the dozens of other dramatic slopes. Passing the Sprauve Elementary School on her left, she noticed kids playing soccer at recess. Did they know how lucky they were that their lives were so simple? She hadn't back when she'd played hoops at the public school in Allerton where she attended grade school.

Without thinking about it, Sabrina turned and headed toward Bar None. Neil would know what she should do about the necklace. Maybe it wasn't fair to ask him for advice when Detective Hodge was already scrutinizing him for overstepping legal boundaries, but Hodge didn't have to know. Maybe she could give it to Neil and have him put it in the Bar None safe. No, that was a really crazy idea that could result in them being cellmates. At the very least, she could use the opportunity to get Lisa a coffee to go, which, by the sound of her snoring, would be a stellar idea. Maybe Neil would give her one of his bear hugs, which she always pretended were too tight but actually made her feel safe and impenetrable.

But Neil's parking spot was empty, so Sabrina drove on, back through Cruz Bay, up Centerline Road, which ran right through the middle of St. John from one end to the other. She took a right at the ridiculously marked "Route 104" where wild goats and pigs roamed, although less so since the island dump was shut down. She headed past the fork in the road, a six-foot metal sculpture cut out in the shape of a fork, and up Gifft Hill Road, where Henry lived. Should she stop and put the necklace in his safe, which they used for Ten Villas? She and Henry had the keys and combinations to each other's locks, safes, homes, and vehicles. They had no secrets, or at least Sabrina had thought they hadn't, which was why it had been a little unsettling to hear Henry confess he'd gone to chat with Elena about the prenup.

Maybe she should drive on out past Villa Nirvana first to her own cottage high up on a hill in Fish Bay and leave the necklace in her own safe. No, the police had gotten search warrants for both her house and Henry's condo the last time there had been a murder in one of their villas.

Sabrina began to feel like she couldn't breathe, a sure sign she was in panic mode. Her cell phone began to play "Locked Away," flooding her with relief because it meant Neil was calling her. She pulled over to the side of the road by the posh Rendezvous Bay neighborhood so she would have reception, just as Lisa jolted upright and awake in her seat. Damn. Sabrina had hoped Lisa would stay asleep long enough so she could speak privately to Neil. Life on an island was filled with draconian choices. If she got out of the car, there was a good chance the call would drop. Hell, even if she stayed still, reception could instantly vanish. Better to have Lisa overhear her conversation than to lose the opportunity to get Neil's advice.

"Hey Salty, David and I've been over to see Cassie and got her blessing to use Larry's plane. We're going over to check it out now and maybe do a little trial run, just so David gets a feel for the plane and does a landing or two. He says it's been about a year since he flew a seaplane over in Culebra."

"That sounds like a good idea. I'm headed over to Villa Nirvana with Lisa Keating to meet the others. Detective Hodge is letting them get their possessions."

"I'll bet he's got more than that in mind. Answer his questions in 'yes' or 'no' responses whenever you can. Do not volunteer any information. Remember, these guys aren't your friends," Neil said while Sabrina nodded a silent "aye, aye" to his instructions.

"Neil, can they search me or my things, like my jeep or my purse, without a search warrant?" Sabrina asked as she watched Lisa's eyebrows arch.

"No, they can't, and I doubt they have one yet, so don't consent to any search. By tomorrow, David and I hope to have some information about Elena that may suggest why someone wanted to kill her. Did you know he's fluent in Spanish?"

Another secret Henry kept from her, although she didn't suppose this one had been intentional.

"Hey, Salty, listen. I'm calling for another reason. David and I reconnoitered your casa a little while ago. It's a good thing you kept the cargo container in front of it," Neil said. Sabrina detected a note of pride in his voice. It had been his gift to her, a full size cargo container, placed in front of her tiny cottage as a barricade against the press, who had come to hunt her down during the murder at Villa Mascarpone several months earlier. Neil wasn't your average almost-boyfriend, and his gifts were proof of it. But wait, why was it good she'd kept the cargo container, which was still under a lease Neil had paid for?

"Neil?" she pressed, wishing Lisa had had three Bloody Marys and was still zonked so she would have some privacy.

"Sorry, kid, but they're back. At least one was parked and hanging out in front of the container. You'd better stay with me tonight on the Knot Guilty."

Neil had never invited her to his home, telling her he was a typical guy-slob, only worse because he lived on a trawler. She wasn't sure if he was really a slob or if he had just been reluctant to share his entire world with her. Sabrina thought the invitation might mark movement in their relationship until she realized he'd only offered because he was concerned about reporters being at her house.

"We'll see," she said, instead of saying no, and hung up.

"How's your head?" Sabrina asked Lisa, who was rubbing her forehead.

"I'm okay. I couldn't help but hear. Are the cops going to be asking us questions?"

"They may be. Why?"

"Because I may want a lawyer if they do," Lisa said.

Chapter Twenty-One

A uniformed police officer stood at the gatehouse at Villa Nirvana. Sabrina stopped the jeep, rolled down her window, and took a deep breath. While she felt better knowing the cops wouldn't likely search her tote bag, she'd rather the necklace be somewhere else entirely. She still wasn't sure what to do. If she left her bag in the car, how would she know if the police searched it without her knowing? And if she took the bag into the house, what would happen if she was separated from it?

"Hi, I'm Sabrina Salter," she said in her most breezy, friendly greeting that she usually reserved for villa guests.

"Yes, I know who you are. Who's she?" the young policeman asked.

"Lisa Keating," Sabrina said as the cop looked at papers attached to a clipboard and waved them through. Sabrina drove up the dirt road, past Ditleff Beach, where just yesterday she had pulled Elena's body out of the water, shivering at the memory of the feel of wet lace and cold, damp skin. Looking at the beach today, Sabrina didn't see a single sign that a woman had died there. The dive team must have come and gone.

The Ten Villas van was parked next to the idle and empty rental jeeps. Sabrina got out of the Ten Villas jeep, quickly opened the back door and reached into her tote bag for the necklace, still in a plastic sandwich bag, and slipped it back into the pocket of her shorts while Lisa exited from the passenger's side. If the necklace was with her, at least she had a modicum of control over what happened to it and to her.

They walked around a half a dozen cruisers parked by the front entrance, essentially as a barricade. Another young uniformed police officer stood at the foot of the small set of stairs like a sentry at a Roman palace. Sabrina made introductions again and walked with Lisa into the great room, where Henry and the Keating entourage sat perched on the rattan sofas and chairs Elena had selected personally with Sean.

To Sabrina, the villa looked like a St. John hurricane had blown through. Past the great room by the pool, the tables that had been so painstakingly set by her staff for the wedding feast were now littered with dirty dishes, glasses, and silverware. Cloth napkins dotted the terra-cotta tiled floors. Several gardenia plants had been toppled with dirt and fading blossoms cascading out of their pots. The ornate mahogany bar, which sat on wheels, had been relocated from the great room to the poolside. Sabrina could see the fully stocked supply of liquor had been almost depleted. The lights above the tables on the tents were still on, even though the midafternoon sun was burning down on the villa.

Sabrina fumed. She had little doubt about what had happened at Villa Nirvana. Sure, there had been some investigating done by the police, but to her, it looked like there had been a whole lot more partying. Debauchery at a crime scene where a wedding should have taken place was bad enough, but at the hands of the police, it was disgraceful.

She looked around at the faces of the Keating clan for any sign they were equally outraged and was surprised to find none. Sean's swollen eyes looked unfocused and dazed. Heather sat at the edge of her chair looking down at the floor, while Kate and Jack sat back on a couch leaning into one another. Even Paul, the understated CFO, appeared to be concentrating at gazing out the window on the opposite side of the room. No one seemed to even notice the disarray surrounding them. Sabrina looked at Henry for a reality check. His subtle frown told her he got it.

"Where is the other brother?" Detective Hodge asked, not bothering to greet her or Lisa. He stood with his arms folded in front of him with a scowl that reminded Sabrina how unpleasant cops could be and how nice it was when one was civilized, like Leon Janquar.

"I don't know." Sabrina figured Lisa could make excuses for Gavin since she had so much experience at it.

"He said he'd meet us all here. He had some business calls to make and the reception at the Westin isn't very good," Lisa said, sinking down on to a couch next to Kate.

"Detective Hodge, these folks have been through an ordeal in the past two days. Can't you just let them get their stuff so we can get them away from here?" Sabrina asked, choosing not to sit down but rather meet Detective Hodge at eye level.

"So you agree that it's not wise to have guests staying at this villa, Miss Salter?" Sabrina could see that Hodge's confrontational tone had caught the attention of the Keatings and Paul Blanchard, all of whom were now focused on her.

"I agree it's not wise to have guests staying here after it has somehow been transformed from a glorious setting for a wedding feast into a pigsty the Board of Health would shut down in a minute. It will take hours for a crew to make this villa habitable again." Sabrina could feel her heart pumping at a rapid rate. She knew she should shut up, but that didn't stop her. She was furious and tired of being afraid of cops who were bullies. Screw it.

Ignoring her, Hodge turned to the others, his back now facing Sabrina.

"My investigative team has worked tirelessly all night and cleared all the rooms on the main floor, including your bedrooms, with the exception of the victim's room on the upper level. I have a list of items we have confiscated as evidence. If you find something missing in your room as you pack your belongings, you may check with me."

"Why would anything be missing from our rooms? You can't just seize people's stuff." Gavin swaggered into the great room as if he were the chairman of the board.

"Oh, but I can, Mr. Keating. So nice of you to join us."

Sabrina was relieved that Gavin seemed to have captured Detective Hodge's vitriol, replacing her as a target.

"What's going on? Lisa said you were making business calls. I'm out of the loop without my cell phone, which I certainly hope isn't on your list Detective Hodge," Jack said.

"I have mine, but I haven't gotten any messages about anything going on," Paul said.

Sean shook his head.

"I don't even have my phone on."

"They're only calling me. I listed my number as the contact when I issued the press release yesterday. I didn't think Sean would be up to it, and neither of you have ever enjoyed contact with the press, so I stepped up to the plate," Gavin said.

Sabrina marveled at how he had managed to turn a police investigation into a business meeting. The guy was smooth.

"Who's calling you?" Heather asked.

"A number of reporters. Apparently someone leaked the information that Elena was murdered," Gavin said, looking directly at Hodge.

"I think you should just respond to any inquiry with 'no comment.' No good can come to Keating Construction, or to any of us for that matter, from the press." Jack leaned forward.

"I agree," Paul said.

"Well, I don't. We need to make sure this doesn't work against the company. I mean, here we have an in-house wedding between a high-ranking employee and the son of the owner, and the bride gets murdered the night before the wedding. You don't think *Inside Edition*, *People Magazine*, and *Chasing Justice* will be all over this? We either spin it to our advantage or get run over with it. You have to be one step ahead of these vipers."

Sabrina almost gagged at Gavin's pomposity. Lecturing his father and the company CFO, Gavin's voice was tinged with arrogance. What had a nice girl like Lisa ever seen in such a jerk?

"Okay, folks. Enough company business. Why don't you all go pack your belongings and then come back here so I can start the interviews," Detective Hodge said, apparently also having had enough of Gavin as the rest of them.

Gavin sat down in an empty chair as the others rose to go to their rooms.

"Don't you have personal items here you wish to retrieve, Mr. Keating?" Hodge asked.

"My wife will get them for me, Detective," Gavin said, looking over toward the pool where the sun was beginning to relent. "Holy shit, what the hell happened there?"

he said, rising to his feet and pointing at the tables strewn with dirty dishes and other debris from the wedding feast.

Hodge didn't bother answering him. Sabrina sat next to Henry and waited in silence while Gavin scrolled down his phone and answered e-mails. Within twenty minutes, everyone had returned to the room, rolling suitcases behind them. Henry jumped to help Lisa drag three small pink ones and two additional adult-size suitcases.

"Does anyone need to check the list to see if they're missing any items that have been retained to help us with our investigation?" Hodge asked, pulling a folded sheet of lined yellow legal paper from the breast pocket of his shirt.

"I'd like to see the list," Lisa said, walking over to take it from Detective Hodge. She scanned it and gave it back, obviously not pleased by what she had seen or perhaps not seen.

"Gavin, you really ought to open your own suitcase to make sure you have everything."

Gavin looked up from his phone.

"What? Why? You're the one who packed it."

"May I just double check?" Heather asked, reaching to take the paper from Hodge. Sabrina was dying to see what was on the list.

Heather looked up from the paper.

"Why did you take my flip-flops? And it looks like everyone else's. And my mother's art supplies."

"To identify various footprints along the beach, of course. And because the art supplies were near the scene of the murder," Hodge said, a smug smile on his face. He liked being in control just as much as Gavin Keating did.

"There's no jewelry on this list," Heather said.

"Why? Are you missing any jewelry, Miss Malzone?"

"Dr. Malzone," Henry said, speaking for the first time.

"I don't know. I can't remember what I packed," Heather said, handing the list back to Hodge.

"Now that everyone has collected their items, we can start the interviews. Miss Salter and Mr. Whitman, I'll be taking you last, so feel free to start cleaning up," Detective Hodge said, motioning toward the tables. Sabrina's jaw dropped, but a glance from Henry told her not to take the bait.

"Sorry, but I've got a five o'clock appointment I can't miss," Gavin said, finally standing to take one of the suitcases Lisa and Henry had deposited in front of him.

"I'm not going to be interviewed without an attorney, Detective Hodge," Lisa said, taking the children's suitcases and wheeling the other adult one over to her husband.

"None of us are." Jack looked over at Paul, who nodded in agreement.

"Neil Perry is securing counsel for me. You know that. He told you that yesterday," Sean said, sounding more alert than he had all afternoon. "And if you expect me to spend sunset in this house, sir, you are going to have to arrest me."

Chapter Twenty-Two

Sabrina practically skipped to the area where the four rental jeeps were parked. The minirevolt launched by Gavin resulted in Detective Hodge issuing a stern warning that "Each of you must report to police headquarters at nine on Tuesday morning to be interviewed—with or without attorneys."

"Sean wants his own jeep so he can go find Neil," Henry said, grabbing the keys to a bright-orange Wrangler from Sabrina, who handed him a form for Sean to sign.

"Heather and I would like one so we can go grocery shopping and pick up food for dinner. We don't feel much like going out. And if there's some place on island that sells art supplies, I'd love to know," Kate said.

"Art supplies? There are a number of places you can get them. This island is crawling with artists." Henry took out one of the St. John guide maps from the glove compartment and marked locations for her.

"We'll take a jeep and a map that shows where you can buy some decent bourbon and cigars," Jack said, while Paul scrawled his signature for Sabrina on the rental form.

"How about you, Lisa? Do you want a ride back to the Westin or a rental jeep of your own?" Sabrina asked as she gazed at Gavin driving away alone in his mother's rental jeep in the distance.

"I guess I'd better have my own jeep at this point," Lisa shrugged as the others pulled away behind Henry's van, which was leading them to town. Sabrina wanted to get away from Detective Hodge before his fury at them for asserting their rights got the best of him, but she couldn't resist asking Lisa what led her to insist on having counsel present during an interview with the police.

"Are you kidding? After I heard the go-round between Detective Hodge and my mother-in-law last night, I am terrified of that man," Lisa said.

"I didn't know about that. What happened?" Sabrina asked. She'd wondered if Detective Hodge and Sergeant Detree might head over to the Westin after hearing Kate suggest the signature they had been asked to identify was Anneka's.

"He and a female officer banged on the door until he woke up everyone in the condo, including the kids. Gavin was furious, but Detective Hodge demanded to speak to Anneka alone in the kitchen," Lisa said.

"Did she agree?" Sabrina asked.

"You don't know my mother-in-law very well, do you?" Lisa chuckled.

"I've only met her once, not under ideal circumstances."

"With Anneka, there are no ideal circumstances. The only people she treats with less than brute force are her granddaughters, fortunately. But with everyone else she's a relentless tyrant. She told Hodge he had no business bullying an elderly visitor in the middle of the night and that she intended to lodge a complaint against him. Why was she being intimidated to identify a signature at such an ungodly hour, which certainly could wait until morning? I will say, she gave Hodge a run for his money."

"Did he back down?" Sabrina asked, wishing she could have seen the contest between Hodge and Anneka Lund, not sure she could root for either.

"No, but he dialed it down a bit and cajoled her by saying surely, she must understand his concern when a beautiful bride was murdered on the island on the eve of her wedding, particularly when Anneka's own son, his wife, and her grandchildren had been staying at the scene of the crime," Lisa told her as she signed the rental form Sabrina had given her.

"So, did she admit it was her signature?" Sabrina cut to the chase so they could get off the Villa Nirvana property if Hodge was tempted to come out and detain her, or even to demand she clean up after his food orgy.

"Of course not. She said she was too tired, had taken a sleeping pill, and couldn't be positive it was her signature. She told him she would have to see the entire document after she got some sleep and after she contacted her attorney to be present with her. Hodge got nervous when he heard that. These island cops don't seem to like getting lawyers involved. That's why I knew to demand one." Lisa had the keys in the ignition now, the car running with the air conditioner turned up full blast. She seemed hesitant to leave.

"Sabrina, the necklace I told you about, the one Gavin is giving me for our anniversary, it wasn't in our room and it wasn't on Hodge's list. Do you think, would the cops take it? I mean, would they steal it?" Lisa asked.

Would one of the island cops steal an expensive diamond necklace during a search? Lee Janquar wouldn't. Sabrina didn't think Lucy Detree would either, from what she had observed of her. The cops who had helped solve Carter Johnson's murder months before had seemed honest. But Sabrina believed Hodge and the crew who had basically looted the Villa Nirvana wedding feast, including the liquor and wedding cake, were capable of stealing from guests. But she knew that, in this case, they hadn't and that the necklace Lisa was concerned about was sitting in the pocket of her shorts. She wanted to tell Lisa not to worry, the necklace was safe with her, but couldn't and felt the weight of one piece of jewelry was more than she could bear. She needed to get rid of it and fast.

"I don't know, Lisa. There could be a lot of explanations for where the necklace is. But for now, what's important is that you and I get as far away from Villa Nirvana and Detective Hodge as fast as we can."

Chapter Twenty-Three

Neil sat in the booth at Bar None that he had claimed as his office. With the rattan shades drawn down, he could escape both the late afternoon sun and the curiosity of his patrons. Visitors to St. John seemed to have endless interest about what it was like to live on an island. He'd fielded enough questions since he'd moved there. Now he had some of his own. What exactly was he doing, living on St. John? Had he chosen the road less traveled only to find himself heading back to the path he'd jumped off?

He had enjoyed his day with David. Even the first slightly rocky landing David had made in the harbor in Charlotte Amalie had been fun. Planning their trip to San Juan to explore Elena's past had exhilarated Neil. Adventure, was that what he needed? Was the peace and tranquility he sought in St. John extinguishing his sense of spirit?

He caught sight of Sean Keating entering Bar None through the cracks in the rattan shades. He was glad all his bartenders were back so that he didn't have to worry about staffing the bar while the murder at Villa Nirvana was still under investigation.

Neil lifted the shade and motioned Sean to come over. Sean looked like he had aged a decade in the past thirty-six hours.

"How did it go over at Villa Nirvana?" Neil asked.

"Seriously, I thought the cops in LA were jerks." Sean summarized what had happened, including the mass exodus after a unified demand for counsel.

"Good job," Neil said, calling over for Mitch to bring them a couple of St. John Brewers Amber Jacks.

"Look, Neil, the truth is I do need a lawyer. You warned me how this could go, and seeing how ruthless Hodge and his so-called team are, I'm totally convinced. I'm also not sure what's been going on in my family and in the family business in particular." Sean accepted a mug of beer from Mitch and took a swig.

"Nice," he said.

"Local microbrewery. Now tell me what you mean about the family and family business."

"I'm not really sure. But since Elena passed, it feels like Gavin has started to take over the whole operation. He's making decisions on his own, claiming that he's trying to be sensitive to my loss, and pretty much ignoring my father and Paul. He's hell-bent on the company's reputation not being affected by Elena's murder. It's just so cold-blooded."

"Did he and Elena get along?"

"Sure. Gavin was the one who hired Elena, so of course she liked him. She said she admired what she called Gavin's 'savage business savvy.' He never let emotions stand in the way of business decisions. She told me I should develop a sense of detachment instead of being so hotheaded. The only time I saw them disagree about anything big was about the prenup," Sean said, taking another gulp of beer. "Damn, this is good. Can I have another?"

Neil leaned over and called to Mitch again, asking for a refill for Sean only. He was meeting Sabrina in a half hour and needed to pace his drinking, plus he had a full day tomorrow.

"Sean, what do you know about Elena's life as a kid in San Juan, other than the part about being poor and the explosion?" Neil asked.

"Nothing. She didn't like to talk about it. Once when we were in San Juan on business, I asked her if she'd like to show me the *caserio* and talk a little about what it was like for her when she lost everyone in the explosion and fire. I asked about the friend she was doing the school project with and if they kept in contact."

"Did they?" Neil asked.

"No. All Elena said was that her friend had been like an angel to her. I pressed a little more. I wanted to be sensitive about how different her childhood and mine were. She had come to the house where I grew up in Tiburon, where my parents still live. She had met them socially and spent some holidays there. I felt a little bad there was nothing left of her family to share with me."

"Did she open up?"

"No. I even talked a little about what it was like to grow up in a family where a bitter divorce caused constant hard feelings. I told her how Gavin had been jealous of me and even of Heather because we got to live with his father. How he would lie and try to get me in trouble for the things he did and when he got caught would complain to his mother, which meant my mother got involved. I thought Elena might feel better if she didn't think we had been the perfect family and would understand that I didn't mind if hers hadn't been either. But it didn't work. She told me the past was the past and I should just move on like she had."

"That's kind of interesting. The guy encouraging the woman to talk about her feelings." Neil considered what a profound effect Elena had had on Sean.

"Elena was different from any other woman I ever dated, Neil. She changed how I thought about everything—business, marriage, family, sex, love. I want to know who did this to her and why. I don't want this story to become the next national spectacle broadcast on Fox News. That much I agree with Gavin on. I hope you can find some answers tomorrow."

"I do, too, Sean. I really do. I hesitate to ask the most difficult question, but you know I am a straight shooter. Do you have any question in your mind that someone in your own family who was at Villa Nirvana that night might have killed Elena?"

"No, not at all. Three of them are older people, ready to retire, who just wanted to see me happy. Heather is my sister and a chiropractor. She loves me and is a healer. No way she would do this. Lisa doesn't have a mean bone in her body. Even Gavin would never risk the business by getting involved in something criminal."

Neil looked out through the slats in his blinds and noticed a couple sitting at the bar, deep in conversation.

"Well, maybe he won't go so far as to commit a crime, but from here it looks like he's willing to sleep with the enemy. I suggest you slip out of my office through the rear door here. It seems your half brother is being interviewed at the bar by an INN reporter. That means Faith Chase is on the story."

Chapter Twenty-Four

Sabrina rushed past the road that led to her cottage, knowing there might still be a news crew there. Would she always need to fear and avoid cops and reporters? When she had been a television meteorologist, she interacted with reporters every day. There were some talented and tireless investigative journalists who she admired and with whom she worked side by side in blizzards and hurricanes. But sensational crimes seemed to attract the pond scum of the media, and no crime was more sensational than murder.

Winding up the dirt road that overlooked Reef Bay, Sabrina realized how much she missed her dog. Girlfriend brought routine and normalcy to her life. Their nightly swims were Sabrina's favorite part of the day, made even more so when Neil joined them.

She pulled into the driveway of the Banks' home, appreciating how the hibiscus hedge was always meticulously trimmed. She respected Evan Banks for not giving in to the Alzheimer's disease, which was making him slowly slip away. She admired even more how his wife, Lyla, worked to help him hold on.

Lyla barely had the front door open when Girlfriend leapt to greet Sabrina. Sabrina laughed out loud as the dog kept jumping and landing kisses on her face and neck. Was there anything better than being loved by a dog?

"She's missed you, dear," Lyla said, stepping back into the house to let Sabrina enter.

"And we'll miss her. Any time you need someone to watch her, you know who to call." Evan gathered Girlfriend's overnight bag, which Sabrina had filled with food and toys before dropping her off the day of the wedding rehearsal. It was just two days before, but it felt like a month to her.

"Do you have time for an ice tea?" Lyla asked.

"I wish I could, but it turns out the bride's death wasn't accidental, and it's created a bit of a mess for Henry and me." Sabrina wished she could sit and chat over ice tea and not have to worry about how another murder had landed in Ten Villas' lap.

"We know. It's all over the news. I hope you're not taking it personally," Lyla said.

"Don't listen to that bore. Blaming Ten Villas for poor security is ridiculous. Everything is always someone else's fault. It's common knowledge murders are most often committed by family members," Evan said.

Sabrina liked it when Evan sounded off. He was such an intelligent man. Alzheimer's was a cruel disease.

"Wait, what bore? What are you talking about?" Sabrina realized she hadn't fully comprehended Evan's comment.

"The brother of the groom. He talked about the irony of the tragedy. He said his family was launching a new villa construction business, only to have his brother's bride murdered the night before her wedding because the villa management company had shoddy security. I'm sorry. If it helps, he sounded like an arrogant prig."

Lyla reached over to take Sabrina's hand in hers. "I hate to add to your burden, Sabrina, but I think you'd better check in on your guests across the street at Villa Mascarpone. The husband came over a little while ago to ask if we had a break-in, too."

"A break-in? Just what we need. I'm sorry. Did they have a break-in? Did you?" Sabrina couldn't imagine what else could creep into this very long and disastrous day.

"Not with your watchdog. No one would dare come near us with that noble beast on the premises," Evan said.

"No, we're fine. But apparently the Hewitts had a visit from the so-called skinny-dippers and are upset. I hope you don't mind, but I told them you were coming to pick up Girlfriend and that I'd have you stop by," Lyla said.

Sabrina had the irrational urge to tell Lyla that she had no business putting one more item on her plate. She had surpassed her quota for unpleasant tasks for one day, and this next one was well past her limit. Now she would have to put on the Ten Villas smile and voice to calm the Hewitts down. Where was Henry when she needed him? He was the one with the charm and diplomacy, not her. She took a deep breath and bit her tongue, knowing Lyla was the messenger, not the message.

"Thanks, Lyla. I'll stop by on my way out. Funny, but I think this is the first time the skinny-dippers have hit a villa that is occupied. I've been under the impression they chose unoccupied ones." Sabrina considered how what had seemed like a series of innocent pranks could become ugly if there was a confrontation with villa guests.

Sabrina called "Inside" at the periwinkle blue gate before unlatching it and walking to the pool area, where she would never be able to enter without picturing the dead body of a man in the hammock hanging below the pergola. Months had passed since Carter Johnson's murder, but Sabrina still had nightmares about finding his body and the investigation of the murder, which had almost ended her new life on St. John. Was this second murder a message? Did she not belong here?

"So glad to see you, Sabrina," Martin Hewitt said, opening the sliding screen doors that led into the house.

Sabrina walked past the pool where the signature hibiscus was floating on the surface. In the living room, Vicki Hewitt was sitting in a chair with a half-empty martini glass on the end table next to her. Her expression told Sabrina the skinny-dippers were no longer funny.

"It's pretty unsettling to be vacationing in paradise, doing a little shopping at Mongoose Junction, and hear a bride had been murdered the night before her wedding.

But then to return to your villa to find a couple of fat naked people climbing out of the pool, well it's scary," Vicki's voice trembled as she downed what was left of her martini.

"Did you see their faces?" Sabrina asked.

"That would have been merciful, but no, we only saw their naked butts," Martin said.

"I'm so sorry," Sabrina told them and she was. She could see how the skinny-dippers seemed bizarre at best, but when considered along with the fact a murder had happened on such a small island, the incident could feel frightening.

Sabrina explained that the anonymous skinny-dippers had been pulling their pranks for a few weeks and were considered harmless, although annoying.

"Did you report this to the police or shall I?" she asked, relieved to hear the Hewitts had not.

"I'll take care of it right away for you. And I'll have our local locksmith come out and reset the combination on the locks for you. Is there anything else I can do?"

Having appeased the guests, Sabrina got into her jeep, happy to have Girlfriend riding shotgun again. She pulled away down the steep curve until she found a spot with cell phone reception where she pulled over to make a call. The last number she was going to call was the police.

Chapter Twenty-Five

Henry looked down at his cell phone. The caller ID said Sabrina.

"I have to take this call," he told David, who was sitting opposite him, looking at the menu and drinking a frozen painkiller.

David nodded, immersed in the menu.

Henry stepped outside the restaurant onto the street so he could hear.

"Where are you? I can barely hear you," Sabrina said.

"At Sushi Sunday at the Longboard. With David. He's taking me out for dinner. I chose the restaurant."

"Oh. Nice."

"Not necessarily. David hates sushi," Henry said.

"Henry."

He recognized that tone his mother used as a warning when he was a kid.

"He said 'whatever it takes.' Besides, he wanted to cook for me at his cottage."

"That was nice."

"You've never eaten his cooking. Plus, I don't want to see him other than in a public setting. You understand?" Henry wasn't even sure if he wanted to see David at all, but with the way he'd become insinuated into the investigation, Henry had to be civil.

"Listen, we've got another problem out at Villa Mascarpone, Henry."

"Shit. Do not tell me if another person has gotten himself murdered. The body count on this island is already too high." Henry hated how out of control his life was beginning to feel.

"Relax, it's not that bad. But it is unsettling." Sabrina explained how the skinny-dippers had gone to Villa Mascarpone, even though it was occupied.

"I get why the Hewitts are upset. I'm a little freaked at this point by these creeps and everything else going on in St. John, aren't you?" Henry asked.

"Of course, but it's bigger than that, Henry. The Hewitts wanted me to report it to the cops. Do you know what would happen if Detective Hodge heard that the skinny-dippers trespassed on one of our properties that was occupied? He'd probably shut down all ten of our villas and we would be out of business. Picture explaining that to our villa owners." Henry could hear the panic in her voice and was reminded that they wouldn't be part of this mess if he hadn't been so adamant about adding Villa Nirvana.

"What can I do?"

"Can you get Billy over to change the lock combinations and keys tonight? Tell him we'll pay double since it's Sunday," Sabrina said, signing off.

Henry made the call to Billy Wiggs, who was more than happy to earn double the money for an easy job, and then returned to the table, where he could see David had started a new painkiller.

"Everything okay?" David asked.

"Just a little business problem. It's all set. So how did it go with Neil and Cassie?"

"Great. It's a terrific little plane. Larry kept it in great shape. Neil and I took it out and other than the first landing, which was a little rough, I think I've got my mojo back. I felt bad for Cassie. You guys are having a rough week here on St. John. But I'm impressed with how everyone seems to pull together on an island."

"Yes, we're a tight community." Henry closed his menu.

"Cassie asked me if I'd like to buy Larry's plane."

"What did you tell her?"

"I said maybe. Then she said she'd give me a deal if I bought the house with it. She wants to go back to Florida, where her kids and grandkids are."

A shiny-faced server with long legs in short shorts named Kayla appeared at the table to take their order.

Henry ordered a Spicy Island sushi roll.

"Why don't we just share the Sashimi Sampler Plate?" David asked.

"Why would we do that? You'd love the Island Wings they make here. You hate sushi." Henry said, not sure if he was more thrown by David's news that Cassie had offered to sell Larry's plane and their house or by David ordering sushi.

"Whatever it takes, Henry." David raised his glass in a toast.

Chapter Twenty-Six

Sabrina decided to check her messages before she lost reception.

"Meet me in the rear parking lot at St. John Car Rental. Do NOT come to Bar None. N.P."

Just what she needed. The number of places she couldn't go on St. John was growing at an alarming rate. Her world couldn't afford to shrink much smaller. She was already living on an island that was less than three-by-nine miles.

She drove up the near perpendicular hill that led to the parking lot where Neil was waiting. She grabbed her tote and Girlfriend's overnight bag from the backseat while Girlfriend peed over by the bushes. She walked over to Neil's jeep, whistling for Girlfriend as she opened the back passenger door. The dog dove in, rushing toward Neil in the front seat, showering him with kisses on his neck and ears.

"Geez, Salty, I wish you'd take a page from your dog and learn how to properly greet a man," Neil said, laughing as Sabrina pried the dog off him. He leaned over and gave her a peck on the check. They were still at that awkward stage where they weren't quite sure how to act when they met each other.

"Why couldn't I go to Bar None, Neil? What's going on?" She had little patience for small talk with so much at stake.

"Relax, we just had that reporter I saw admiring your cargo container at the bar chatting with Sean's brother. I didn't think you'd want to run into them. Besides, I'm in the mood for a Skinny Legs cheeseburger. How about you?"

"Sure, that sounds great." Sabrina realized how hungry she was, not having eaten a meal since the disassembled wedding feast the night before.

She took the twenty-minute ride from Cruz Bay to Coral Bay to tell Neil about the diamond necklace still in her pocket.

"Oh, now I get why you were asking me questions on the phone about searches. Why didn't you just tell me what was going on?" Neil asked.

"Because Lisa was sitting in the car next to me."

"So let me see if I've got this straight. You found the diamond necklace in Heather's pocket in the laundry and put it in a baggie in your pocket for safekeeping. You forgot to return it to Heather when things got heated at Bella Vista. When you go to bring Lisa over to Villa Nirvana, she tells you that she found a diamond necklace in Gavin's toiletry bag, which she believes is an anniversary gift that

Gavin is planning to give her. But when Hodge lets everyone retrieve their belongings, Lisa doesn't find the necklace in with Gavin's stuff and it's not on the list of items confiscated by the police. Have I got that right, Salty?"

"Yes, and then Heather comments that there's no jewelry on the list, but doesn't admit she's missing anything."

"And all that time, the necklace is in your pocket?"

"Yes."

"How do these things keep happening to you?" Neil asked, pulling into a parking space in the rugged lot at Skinny Legs.

"Are you saying that I'm doing something to cause bad things to happen to me? All I did was wash the Keatings' laundry so they would have clean clothes to wear. It's not like I tried to insert myself into their situation. I was just trying to be considerate," Sabrina said, while Girlfriend tried to climb into the front seat, hearing the plaintive tone in her owner's voice.

"Salty, Salty, listen to me. Don't bite my head off. I'm not accusing you of anything. I'm just trying to help you, honey," Neil said, placing a hand on each of Sabrina's cheeks, looking directly at her.

"I just didn't know what to do."

"Let's feed you and then we can decide."

Sabrina felt like a new woman after two lemon vodkas and an almost-raw blue cheeseburger. With Girlfriend at her feet and Neil next to her on the wooden bench, she was ready to talk about the necklace.

"Let's wait until we get over to my place to sort it out. There's something about being on the water that makes everything seem easier," Neil said.

They fetched Sabrina and Girlfriend's bags and headed to the rickety dock where Neil's inflatable sat. Girlfriend lost her reluctance to board once Sabrina was seated. And within five minutes, Sabrina was boarding the forty-two-foot trawler Neil called home.

Sabrina wasn't sure what she'd been expecting, but it certainly wasn't the painstakingly stained and polished woodwork throughout the boat, which Neil explained was called "bright work." There was a small galley with a stove, microwave, and a refrigerator. In the salon, a built-in couch with lots of pillows sat below a bay of windows. A small, worn Oriental rug was placed before it. On the other side of the trawler was a built-in table with four seats. On top of the table, there was a coffee mug and a book titled *Uniform Commercial Code.*

"See, I told you I was a slob," Neil said, grabbing the mug and book off the table. He put the mug in the sink and the book on a table upside down.

"Are you kidding me? This is gorgeous."

Neil showed her the main cabin in the rear of the boat, where he had removed the berth and had converted it into a study of sorts with a minibar and two leather chairs, which looked like they may have come from his law office. The front stateroom had a typical v-berth where a couple of cotton quilts lay tousled on the beds.

He made her a lemon vodka on the rocks, taking two lemons from his backpack, which he must have brought from Bar None, giving her drink a generous squeeze. She was touched by his thoughtfulness. Neil grabbed a cold bottle of Guinness out of the refrigerator and led her over to the table.

"Okay, what do you want to do about the necklace?" he asked.

"I'd love to be honest and just hand it over to the police."

"Next choice. That would be legal suicide, Salty. You're not dealing with a cop like Lee Janquar here."

"I want to live in a world where I don't have to be afraid of telling the truth," Sabrina said, knowing she was getting just a little drunk.

"We can philosophize about utopian societies when all of this is said and done. Going to Hodge and telling the truth isn't an option. You could try going to Heather and telling her the truth. You could return the necklace and let her figure out what to do with it."

Sabrina smiled. Neil was brilliant. She could be honest and unload the necklace on the person in whose clothes she had found it.

"Of course, that could pose another problem," he said.

She didn't want to hear it, but she knew he would tell her anyway, so she asked.

"What's that?"

"Heather could be dangerous if she's implicated in Elena's death," Neil said.

"But I wouldn't confront her like that, Neil. I could just be honest and say I found it in the laundry. She can talk about it or just thank me. I won't press her."

"If you're comfortable, go ahead and do it. Just make sure other people are around when you do." Neil said, reaching over for her hand. "I'm getting used to hanging around with you, Salty, and I don't want to see anything happen to you."

Sabrina was sober enough to recognize this was as close to a declaration of affection from someone like Neil Perry she might ever get. She squeezed his hand, wanting him to know she also cared deeply for him, but also needing to take a little control over her life, which had been like a plane flying through endless turbulence lately.

"I'll even take Girlfriend with me. I'll go up to Bella Vista after I drop you and David at the plane in the morning."

"Which is coming soon, so we'd better turn in." He took her by the hand he was already holding and steered her into the front stateroom, where he handed her one of the quilts and a pillow, signaling that he understood this was a night when sleep was needed more than sex and that it was okay for them to each sleep on their own berth. Sabrina stretched out, surprised at how comfortable a bed on a boat was, hearing Girlfriend lower herself to the floor between Neil and her. The last thing she remembered was wondering whether Neil or the dog was snoring.

Chapter Twenty-Seven

It was still dark the next morning when Sabrina drove Neil to Gibney Beach, where they picked David up. Both men were quiet during the short ride to Cruz Bay. She wished them good luck on their mission as she dropped them off at the dock next to the ramp Larry used to access his seaplane. Girlfriend slithered over the center console into the front passenger seat next to Sabrina.

She returned Neil's jeep to the empty space at Bar None and retrieved her own from the parking lot at St. John Car Rental, which wasn't open yet. Not much in Cruz Bay was. The morning light was just beginning to illuminate the sky. School children in pink-and-maroon uniforms rushed toward the dock to catch the ferry to St. Thomas where they attended school. Day laborers sat on a concrete wall hoping to be chosen for a day's work.

Life goes on, Sabrina thought. In one weekend, a good man is killed in a car accident. A bride is murdered before her wedding. But come Monday morning, people go back to work. Kids return to school. She took some comfort in the return to normalcy, hoping that Neil and David would find some information that could give answers about Elena. The sound of a plane over Cruz Bay comforted her because she knew they were on their way.

Ten Villas needed to get back on track. They had guests departing several villas over the next few days and replacements arriving. There was cleaning to be done, including the huge mess out at Villa Nirvana.

She called Henry to see if he wanted to meet her for breakfast at Jake's, a favorite meeting place for them where they could enjoy coffee and eggs while they talked business. Breakfast at Jake's would feel normal.

"Sweetie, you should probably keep a low profile until things get sorted out. Come on up here and I'll make you an omelet," Henry said, reminding her normal would have to wait.

She smelled the coffee from outside the front door. Henry greeted her with a hug, something he was always doing whether she wanted one or not. Sabrina wasn't much of a hugger, but between Henry and Neil that had been changing.

"How was your date?" Sabrina asked.

"It wasn't a date. It was dinner. I was just being civilized. David did agree to fly Neil to San Juan, after all."

Sabrina decided to let it go. They were discussing who would do what during the next several days and that her next stop was to see how the Keatings were doing up at

Bella Vista when she realized Henry knew nothing about the necklace. Should she tell him? He was her business partner, but was this a business decision? Did he deserve to know or would it burden him? Would she feel better if she told him? Why did she have to torture herself over such a simple question?

Two bites into a ham and Gruyère cheese omelet and a half a cup of French roast coffee raised Sabrina's blood sugar enough that she was finally thinking clearly. Of course she should tell Henry about the necklace. He wasn't just her business partner. He was also her friend. Her dear friend.

She explained about finding the necklace then not knowing how to get rid of it after she forgot to return it to Heather the day before.

"Well, whatever you do, don't tell Detective Hodge you have it. He'll have you in the slammer before you can say 'not guilty.'"

"I'm going to return it to Heather and not worry why she had it in her pocket. Unless she wants to talk about it. Then I'll listen," Sabrina said.

"She was really down yesterday when I spoke to her. She thinks Elena's death has changed her family forever."

"She's probably right. I doubt Sean will ever be the same. That Gavin is a piece of work. I suppose you know he's claiming to an INN reporter that Ten Villas failed to provide adequate security at Villa Nirvana, which is why a murder happened there," Sabrina said, looking at Henry to see if he knew. His expression told her he did not.

"Are you kidding me? What an asshole. I'd say he's the one with the best motive to kill Elena because he was the most upset that she wouldn't sign the prenup. Even Heather won't rule him out."

Sabrina and Henry exchanged to-do lists, then she drove out to Bella Vista with Girlfriend, which was item number one on her list.

Kate was in the orchid garden, perched on a chair in front of an easel next to a blossom, which was just opening. Sabrina called over to say hello.

"Come tell me what's going on, Sabrina," Kate said.

"Not much." Sabrina didn't want to spoil Kate's art session by tattling on her wicked stepson, although she was tempted. She liked Kate enough that she could put her on her list of "Women I Wouldn't Mind Having for a Mother." Ruth had been the first woman to go on the list, but she had died long ago. She had a couple of teachers who made the list. Lyla Banks had earned a spot. Sabrina had learned that when your own mother deserts you, you have to get your mothering where you can.

"Where is everyone?" Sabrina asked, not wanting to get maudlin.

"Jack and Paul are in town calling the corporate lawyers about getting us representation for our meeting with Detective Hodge. I told them they better call John

Grisham if we're going to have to tangle with that beast. Sean's off on another walk. He needs time alone and seems to like exploring the paths up here. It's really a more interesting property than Villa Nirvana, isn't it?"

"Bella Vista is one of my favorites," Sabrina agreed. "Where's Heather?"

"Reading by the pool. Not having her glasses was worse for her than me not having my paints. She loves to read."

Sabrina found Heather wearing a large brimmed straw hat, with a towel covering most of her fair-skinned body, lounging on a chaise with a book on her lap. She called out softly to Heather so she wouldn't startle her. Heather looked up from *Don't Stop the Carnival.*

"This guy nails it, doesn't he?"

For a moment, Sabrina didn't know what she was talking about but realized Heather was commenting on the book.

"He sure does. The reality of living on an island in the Caribbean is a far cry from the fantasy," Sabrina admitted.

"That's what the villa construction business is all about. Selling a fantasy. It's a lot sexier than building parking garages, I suppose," Heather said.

Sabrina hesitated. Neil had warned her only to confront Heather if there was someone else present, but drawing Kate into what might become an altercation with her daughter seemed unfair and unkind. Besides, she had Girlfriend at her side.

"Heather, I came to return something of yours I found when I did the laundry yesterday. I meant to give it to you when I dropped off the clean clothes, but I got distracted when Sean got upset," Sabrina took the baggie with the broken necklace out of her pocket and handed it to Heather, immediately feeling ten pounds lighter.

Heather looked at the necklace like she had never seen it before and handed it back to Sabrina.

"You must be mistaken. This isn't mine."

"Well, I found it in the pocket of your dress." Sabrina gave the sandwich bag back to Heather.

"Sabrina, I refuse to accept something that is clearly valuable that doesn't belong to me." Heather tossed the baggie to Sabrina, catching her off guard. Instinctively, Sabrina reached out and caught it.

"Listen, I don't know who this necklace belongs to, but it isn't mine and since I found it in your pocket, you can be in charge of where it goes next." Sabrina started to drop the necklace onto Heather's chaise when Heather reached out her arm signaling for her to stop.

"I can appreciate you may be concerned that having such a valuable piece of jewelry that isn't yours could raise certain implications about how you came into possession of it. Maybe you regret something you've done. I wouldn't know. I do know you have a history with the police, but that doesn't mean you can hand the necklace off to me. Why would anyone believe I was carrying a diamond necklace in the pocket of my dress? Seriously, whatever your issue with the necklace is, you're going to have to deal with it better than this and without me." Heather leaned back on the lounge chair, covering her angry red face with *Don't Stop the Carnival*.

Chapter Twenty-Eight

Sabrina was shocked. She had wondered what Heather's reaction to the necklace would be, but she never expected her to suggest that Sabrina might have stolen it. How dare she! She was desperate to talk to Neil, but Sean came off the path and over to the pool, so Sabrina shoved the baggie back into her pocket, furious to have regained possession of it.

"Hey, Sabrina. Did Neil get off okay?" Sean asked. He looked more rested today.

"I saw the plane taking off myself," Sabrina willed herself to sound cheerful for Sean rather than outraged at Heather, who didn't peek out from behind her book. "I'd better get going. I have water for my dog in the car and I've been chatting for ten minutes, which is a long time for a dog in the tropics to go without water, even in the shade."

"Let me grab a bottle of cold water out of the fridge for her and I'll be right out," Sean said.

Sabrina walked to the jeep, grabbing Girlfriend's portable bowl. She checked her phone for messages and saw a text from Neil.

"PR a dead end. Everyone remembers explosion but not the people. Trying city hall next. Wish we had more to go on. Stopping at St. Thomas on way back."

Girlfriend barked as Sean approached the car with three bottles of water. Sabrina gave Girlfriend's bowl to Sean, knowing he would make friends with the thirsty dog this way. He crouched down and before you knew it, Girlfriend was slurping water all over her new pal. Sean laughed as Girlfriend proceeded to nuzzle him.

She hated to spoil the tiny slice of joy Sean was enjoying, but she thought it might be better to cushion him for the disappointment he was in for when Neil and David returned from their unsuccessful mission.

"I got a text from Neil. They're not finding any information about Elena. Lots about the explosion, but nothing specific about the people who were in it or survived," Sabrina said.

"Damn. Why didn't I make her talk more about her life and especially what happened? I tried, but she was so tight lipped about it and I hated making her feel worse. And it was hard. Living in San Francisco, we kept going to places where I'd meet friends from school and I'd have to explain who they were and how I knew them. She was so interested in learning everything she could about me and my life, but she didn't understand that I wanted the same from her."

"Maybe she was embarrassed about how humble her beginnings were compared to yours." Sabrina could understand how Elena might not want to compare notes about growing up poor and without family.

"The only time I heard even an iota about her childhood, beyond the bare facts, was when I introduced her to Angel Pagan at a Giants game." Sean scratched behind Girlfriend's ears, sounding as if he were far away. He should get a dog to help him through this, Sabrina thought. She remembered when Henry had given her Girlfriend and how having a dog had gotten her through the aftershock of what had happened in Nantucket.

"Who's Angel Pagan?" Sabrina asked.

"Not a baseball fan? He's the center fielder for the San Francisco Giants. He grew up in Puerto Rico. The company has season's tickets in the Virgin American Club box and sometimes some of the players will circulate in the boxes before a game. Angel popped into ours and I introduced him to Elena. They spoke a little in Spanish to each other. I could tell that she found the meeting stressful. Elena didn't like spontaneity. She liked to plan things," Sean said.

"Did she know him from Puerto Rico?" Sabrina couldn't grasp why someone would find meeting a baseball player from their homeland stressful.

"Oh no. It was just that his name was similar to the classmate she had been with on the day of the explosion. She had been doing a school project with a girl who was an only child and had a much quieter apartment than Elena, who had five brothers and sisters."

"What was the name of the friend?" Sabrina asked.

"Angelica Pagan. There was another name in the middle that I can't remember. Elena called her 'my little angel.' She said if she hadn't been with Angelica that day, she would have died with her parents and brothers and sister and everyone else in the building, for that matter. And after all that Elena went through to survive, she ends up being murdered. It's not fair. I want to know who did this to her."

The fury in his voice suggested she had better get him back on topic before she lost the opportunity to ask a few follow-up questions. She wondered what it would be like to lose your entire family in an explosion that killed everyone in the entire building. Would you feel guilty for surviving? Sabrina's own meager beginnings in Allerton felt privileged compared to Elena's.

"Did Elena keep in touch with Angelica?" Sabrina asked. She needed to rein Sean and herself in.

"I asked her that. She said Angelica's mother sent Angelica to live in New York with her father, where she would be safe after the explosion."

"Did you share this with Neil?" Sabrina suspected that what Sean had just told her had little value to the investigation, but it was more than what Neil already had to go on. Even a new last name might help. Maybe Mrs. Pagan still lived at the *caserio*.

"I can't remember. I told him about the fire, but I don't think I told him about Elena meeting Angel Pagan." He refilled Girlfriend's empty water bowl with what was left of his own bottle.

Sabrina reached for her cell phone and called Neil, hoping first for reception and second that he and David hadn't left San Juan. For once, luck was with her. Neil picked up, and she quickly imparted the information she had learned to him.

"I know it's not much, but it's something," she said breathlessly to Neil, who told her they would go back to the *caserio*.

"Maybe this will help," Sabrina suggested to Sean, whose eyes she noticed were filling again. She knew only too well what it was like to be flooded with shifting emotions. Sorrow to anger to remorse and back to sadness swept in on relentless waves. The worst part was never knowing where each wave would toss you.

"How will I go on? How can I have a life without Elena? We hadn't even moved into our apartment that she had decorated so carefully. We hadn't taken the cooking classes we both needed because neither of us knew how to cook. We hadn't done so many things she had planned for us, and now we'll never be able to do them."

Tears streamed down Sean's face. Sabrina knew he was about to sob. Why did people feel so comfortable sharing their secrets and their feelings with her, dammit? She had no skills, no words, no nothing to soothe them with. Why couldn't they sense that? Henry told her people opened up to her because she knew how to practice silence, to just be attentive and listen instead of trying to fix their problems. He said she knew how to bear witness.

"Sean, you will always have your memories. No one can take those from you. All those moments when you and Elena were together, especially those when you were alone with her and it felt like there was no one else in the world." Sabrina thought about sleeping next to Neil on his boat the night before, both of them too tired to even contemplate sex, holding hands across their berths while the trawler rocked them to sleep. The sweet moments are what will get Sean through, she thought, until she realized she had unintentionally triggered a deeper grief.

"We hadn't even, even . . ." Sean said. He bent over, sobbing.

Sabrina placed her hand on his back, hoping to rub away the agony and loss in Sean's heart for all he never had and would never have with Elena, which Sabrina now understood included physical intimacy.

Chapter Twenty-Nine

Sabrina was relieved to hear her phone ring, giving her an excuse to leave Sean. That is, until she looked at the caller ID panel and read "VIPD." The last person she wanted to speak to was Detective Hodge. Her conversation with Sean had depleted her. But ducking the call would only delay the agony.

"Ms. Salter, this is Sergeant Lucy Detree."

Sabrina felt like she'd just won the lottery.

"Sergeant Detree, what can I do for you?" While Lucy Detree may carry a badge from the same police department as Detective Hodge, Sabrina's experience with her had been quite different. At her worst, Detree had seemed indifferent, but she had always remained professional.

"I need to meet with you so I can ask some questions, Ms. Salter."

"But Detective Hodge gave everybody until tomorrow morning to retain counsel for our interviews," Sabrina said. She didn't know what she would do if Neil couldn't accompany her to her interview. She knew from experience not to meet with the police without representation.

"It's not really about this case," Sergeant Detree said.

Not really about this case? Was Lucy Detree setting her up? Was she trying to get her to talk without a lawyer? Sabrina wasn't sure. She didn't want to be naive, but she also didn't want to appear uncooperative. Sabrina struggled whenever asked to choose between being a compliant "good girl" or one who knew how to watch out for herself, especially when the line blurred and her survival was linked to her acquiescence to authority. Lucy Detree saved her from herself.

"Look, you can decline to answer any question you'd like until you get a lawyer. I'm just looking for your help."

"When do I have to come to the station?" Sabrina asked.

"You don't. Meet me at Villa Nirvana in an hour," Detree said, hanging up before Sabrina had a chance to respond.

Sabrina dropped Girlfriend off at Henry's condo where she would be cool in the air conditioning. Next, she stopped by Little Olive's food truck to grab a grilled pesto and cheese panini and a lemonade to fortify herself before the appointment.

She drove to Hawksnest Beach, where she miraculously found an empty parking spot. Sabrina took her sandwich and headed for the shade under the pavilion, looking for a brief respite from the Keating saga, only to stumble upon Jack and Paul sitting at a picnic table littered with cell phones, lined yellow legal pads, and a number of empty cans of Carib beer.

"Hey, Sabrina. Come join us," Jack said, waving her over to their table. So much for a moment of quiet reflection. Sabrina trudged over, placing her sandwich and drink on the table.

"Looks like corporate headquarters, Caribbean-style."

"We were just trying to connect with the corporate lawyers to see what they recommend about whether we need representation during our interviews with the police," Jack said. Sabrina could see him eyeing her sandwich. She was starving, even though she had breakfast, but remembered her manners. Ruth had taught her you should always thin the soup for a friend. The Keatings weren't exactly friends, but they were her guests. She took her jackknife off the small tool belt she always wore and cut it into three wedges.

"Here, try a bite of my sandwich. So what did the corporate lawyers say?"

"That they would be happy to come down for a week or two and help us sort it out," Paul said, laughing and shaking his head at the same time.

"This is really good," Jack grinned as a dab of cheese slid down his chin.

"Seriously?" Sabrina asked, handing Jack a napkin. She pictured a team of demanding, uptight corporate lawyers housed at Villa Nirvana. The prospect renewed her annoyance at Henry and his insistence they take on the villa, which she never wanted to step into again. But then she remembered that if Detective Hodge had his way, she never would have to deal with Villa Nirvana or any of their other ten villas again.

"Actually, Gavin had already consulted with them. He authorized them to send a couple of criminal lawyers down here from New York. They're also licensed in the Virgin Islands. This is going to cost the company a bundle," Paul said.

"He shouldn't be acting on his own like that. We've got to rein him in. He's acting like we're already retired, for crying out loud. Geez, we've got at least another three years before he gets to call the shots." Jack took a sip of Carib.

"Yeah, well I doubt we'll be able to retire even then, the way things are going. Can you picture Gavin and Sean running the company without Elena? Talk about oil and water," Paul said, dabbing his mouth with the napkin Sabrina had provided. Even at a picnic table on a beach, he had a commanding presence as if he were sitting at the head of a conference table in a boardroom.

"Was Elena that important to the company? I thought she had only recently started working at Keating Construction," Sabrina asked.

"She was bright enough, for sure. But the real value she brought was bringing balance to the company. And the ability to keep the peace between the brothers," Paul said.

"She had the admiration of my older son, which doesn't happen often, believe me. And she tamed my younger son, which is nothing short of a miracle, according to my wife." Jack opened another can of Carib.

"Elena wasn't like most women, if you'll forgive me for saying. She had a keen sense of business, coupled with an emotional distance, which gave her objectivity. I never saw her be anything but calm and contemplative. Until that night when she became hysterical about the prenup," Paul said.

"She totally lost it. It was like someone else had moved into her body. Bizarre," Jack added.

Chapter Thirty

Sabrina was surprised to find the gate at Ditleff Point open with no police officer manning the gatehouse. Only one police cruiser sat outside Villa Nirvana. Sabrina parked behind it and climbed the short steps to the great room, where Lucy Detree was opening windows and doors. The stench of spoiled food filled Sabrina's nostrils. Dirty plates littered the tables around the room. She gagged as she joined Sergeant Detree in opening the French doors overlooking the pool, where insects had infested the plates left behind by the police.

"Gross," Sabrina said. A variety of bugs dispersed after their feast was interrupted.

"He's disgusting," Lucy Detree muttered under her breath.

"Excuse me?" Sabrina had barely heard Sergeant Detree's words, which could only refer to Detective Hodge.

"It's disgusting," Sergeant Detree said louder.

"Look, I know you want to talk to me, but do you mind doing it while I soak these plates before I need to have an exterminator out here?" Sabrina began stacking plates. She wished she had plastic gloves on.

"Sure." Lucy Detree began making a pile of dishes, to Sabrina's surprise.

They carried the plates into the kitchen and placed them on the counter next to the deep stainless steel double sink. Sabrina ran the hot water from the faucet until it was near scalding, then put the stacks Sergeant Detree handed her into the sinks while she drizzled dish soap over them. Their silent camaraderie disarmed whatever apprehension Sabrina had had about talking to the Sergeant.

"Thank you. Would you like to sit at the counter while we talk? I can probably find some ice tea or seltzer downstairs in the service kitchen if you'd like," Sabrina offered.

"I'm fine," Lucy Detree said, sitting on the same stool Sabrina had found Sean Keating at on the morning that should have been his wedding day. So many things had happened in such a short time. Sabrina felt dizzy. She slid onto the stool opposite the policewoman, grateful to be off her feet, comforted by the soft breeze coming through the windows overlooking Fish Bay.

"Where is everyone else? I thought there would still be police officers here," Sabrina said.

"They released the scene a little while ago. Your people can come back, as long as it's just the owners. No renters. Yet."

Sabrina was encouraged by the word "yet."

"I'll let them know," Sabrina said. She doubted Sean, his parents, or his sister would want to return to Villa Nirvana now or ever. She wouldn't be surprised if the villa went on the market after the murder had been solved.

"Sabrina . . . may I call you that?" Lucy Detree started.

"Of course," Sabrina replied.

"What do you know about the so-called skinny-dippers?"

Sabrina almost fell off her stool. All Lucy Detree wanted to ask her about was the silly skinny-dippers? Well, hallelujah. This was one conversation she didn't mind having with the police.

"They're a pudgy white couple who seem to know when villas are unoccupied. They come and skinny-dip in the pools. Until recently, they'd only been spotted by people in neighboring villas. I saw them myself the night I took the Keatings up to stay in Bella Vista on Bordeaux Mountain. The Ten Villas online availability schedule showed it as unoccupied, so I guess that's why they hit it."

"But none of your occupied villas have been hit?"

"Life has been so crazy, I almost forgot. They hit Villa Mascarpone yesterday. You remember where that is, don't you?" Sabrina asked. She didn't want to mention the murder that took place there just months before for fear of ruining the collaborative tone of the conversation.

"Of course. Go on," Sergeant Detree said.

"The people renting it had been shopping at Mongoose Junction. When they returned to the villa, they apparently interrupted the skinny-dippers." Sabrina was curious why the police were so interested in the annoying, not-so-funny couple when there was a murderer loose on the island, but knew better than to ask.

"Why didn't they report it to us?" Sergeant Detree asked.

Gulp.

"I said I would do it for them." Just when she was building rapport with Lucy Detree, Sabrina realized she had once again stepped on her own feet.

"Is there any reason you didn't?" Sergeant Detree leaned forward, folding her hands on the counter.

"I just forgot. It seemed like a petty crime compared to what happened out here." Sabrina sat back on her stool, resisting the intensity of Sergeant Detree's gaze.

"Sabrina, are there any details about the skinny-dippers' visits to your villas you can remember? Anything else about their appearance or behavior?"

Sabrina sat in silence for a few seconds concentrating on the two occasions she knew about.

"Just that they appear to be middle-aged and chubby. Oh, and they always leave a hibiscus floating in the pool. It's kind of their signature. Maybe a 'Thank you for letting us use your pool.'"

Lucy Detree sat up straight on her stool.

"Hibiscus. You know, I don't see any hibiscus here at Villa Nirvana. Funny, because they are everywhere all over the island," she said.

"The bride wouldn't hear of it. She said they were too 'common.' She liked exotic, fragrant flowers. Gardenias were her favorite. That's why you see them everywhere here. They were the only flowers being used for the wedding. An all-white theme. Elena sure knew what she liked and what she didn't," Sabrina said.

"So finding a red hibiscus blossom in the pool here might be significant."

"Absolutely." Sabrina was astounded by the possibility that the skinny-dippers might be killers.

Chapter Thirty-One

"Why are you still here?" Gavin Keating asked, entering the kitchen as quietly as a cat approaching a mouse.

Sabrina could see Lucy Detree was as stunned by his entry as she had been. Sabrina had never been a fan of surprises, but the Sergeant's displeasure at the sudden sight of Gavin was even more apparent as she rose off her stool and casually moved her hand over her right hip, where her gun holster sat. She stood and faced Gavin squarely.

Rather than back off, Gavin scanned Sergeant Detree from the top of her head down over her body to her feet, then smirked. Sabrina was galled at his audacity.

"Detective Hodge said the crime scene had been cleared. So why are you here, Officer? And why are you here, Sabrina? I thought you'd understand your services are no longer needed since you can't seem to be able to provide the kind of security a villa of this caliber requires," Gavin said.

"Mr. Keating, simply because a crime scene has been cleared does not mean the crime has been solved. A murder still occurred here, and if we need to return to continue our investigation, I assure you that is exactly what we will do. I hope you will cooperate. Obstruction of justice is a serious crime in the Virgin Islands." Sergeant Detree crossed her arms in front of her chest.

"I don't work for you, Gavin. I signed a contract with Sean Keating. Only he can fire me, and I doubt he will." Sabrina rose from her stool, standing next to Lucy Detree.

"Why would he? Ten Villas is a top-notch management company," Sergeant Detree said.

"Well then, why don't you see if you can manage those dirty dishes?" Gavin stormed out of the room.

Sabrina turned to Lucy Detree, who chuckled with her. "Thanks."

"Why is Gavin so upset? What's going on?" Anneka Lund asked, sweeping into the kitchen.

"Why are you here, Mrs. Lund?" Sabrina returned her question with another. She remembered Sergeant Detree ejecting her from Villa Nirvana less than forty-eight hours before. Would she have to do it again?

"Oh relax, Ms. Salter. I'm just here to drop off Gavin with his things. Lisa has his jeep. She's driving the children to the ferry."

Sabrina thought she detected resignation in Anneka's voice.

"Are the children leaving the island?" Sabrina asked.

"Of course. You wouldn't expect Gavin to let them stay on an island where there's a murderer, would you?" Anneka said, now sounding more like the exasperating woman Sabrina had encountered before.

"Lisa Keating isn't leaving St. John, is she?" Sergeant Detree asked warily.

"No, of course not. That dreadful detective made it clear none of us, except the children, can leave. Lisa's mother had to fly down to rescue them. Those poor children will probably be traumatized for life by this experience," Anneka said.

Sabrina wondered if the three sisters even knew what had happened at Villa Nirvana. Lisa had been so adept at protecting them. She suspected they might suffer more ill effects from living with a man like their father.

"Mrs. Lund, I know this has been a nightmare for you and your family, but if people would be a little more forthcoming, we'd have a better chance of solving the case," Sergeant Detree said.

"She's right, Anneka. We all want this to be over and yet we've all hesitated to share information that might be helpful because we don't want to be involved any more than we already are," Sabrina added.

Sabrina watched Anneka look from Lucy Detree to her and back. The wheels were turning.

"Well, people can hardly be encouraged to talk freely when they're spoken to in an accusatory tone by someone who has the authority to arrest them," Anneka said.

Sergeant Detree motioned to an empty stool at the counter where she and Sabrina had been sitting.

"Come sit and have a conversation with me, Mrs. Lund. I need your help."

Anneka hesitated and then moved toward the stool.

"Would you like a cold drink, Anneka?" Sabrina asked, reaching into the refrigerator for a couple of cold bottles of water.

Anneka sat on the stool, placing her forehead on the palms of her hand as if she had a throbbing headache.

"I know you told Detective Hodge you couldn't be sure if it was your signature on the witness line of the document we showed you the other night, but I wonder if you've had time to reconsider. It's no crime to witness a document, so I wouldn't be concerned you're going to implicate yourself in anything illegal."

Anneka sighed.

"How would I know witnessing Elena's signature would subject me to a police interrogation? I was simply in the kitchen at the same time she was."

"Here? You were here with Elena?" Sabrina asked, not able to stop herself.

"Yes. Lisa and Gavin had described the villa and how beautifully it had been decorated for the wedding, I just wanted to peek at it myself. I wasn't invited to the wedding, of course, although I should have been. I am Gavin's mother and it was his half brother who was getting married." Anneka started to take a sip of water. "Do you have a glass?"

Sabrina slid off her stool and retrieved a glass from the cabinet for Anneka.

"Mrs. Lund, when were you here?" Sergeant Detree asked.

"It was well after the rehearsal dinner was over when I figured everyone would be in bed. I never heard the fight about the prenup. I just wanted to get a glimpse of the house and flowers."

Sabrina was surprised to feel a little sorry for Anneka, who sounded lonely and old.

"Where in the house and on the grounds did you go and who did you see? Please, Mrs. Lund. This could be very important." Sergeant Detree's voice was gentle but firm.

"I walked around the great room and the pool area and saw all the lovely gardenias. I couldn't go to any of the bedrooms naturally, so I decided to check out the kitchen. I walked in and found Elena, fully dressed in her bridal gown, barefoot with a bottle of champagne in one hand and a fist full of papers in the other."

"Did you know Elena?" Sabrina asked, even though she knew she should let Lucy Detree ask the questions. She couldn't stop herself.

"I ran into her and Gavin once at a restaurant in Monterey and joined them for dinner. They were at a business conference. I was impressed with her. Smart girl, or so I thought," Anneka said.

"Did something make you change your mind?" Sergeant Detree asked.

"Well, here she was, a little drunk on champagne in her wedding gown and barefoot the night before her wedding, and she wants me to witness her signature on a prenup. She said she was thrilled she didn't have to go down to the media room to ask Lisa or Heather."

Heather was in the media room with Lisa? Why hadn't anyone mentioned that before? Was Heather becoming a bit of a sphinx?

"What did you tell her?" Sabrina asked, although she already was sure she knew the answer.

"Not to sign the damn thing, that's what I told her. No prenup is ever drafted to benefit the person marrying into wealth. That's why I didn't sign one when I married Jack and that's why I didn't get shafted in my divorce." Anneka sounded feisty again.

"What did Elena say?" Sergeant Detree asked.

"That she knew what I was saying was usually true, but in this instance, the prenup was to her benefit. I asked her a few more times if she was sure she wanted to sign it. She kept saying yes, so I witnessed her signature and watched her fold the prenup and place it in a sheet protector. Then, for some unknown reason, she placed it in the refrigerator. It was kind of crazy. I couldn't wait to get out of there. And then . . ." Anneka shook her head and took a sip of water from her glass.

Sabrina and Sergeant Detree looked at each. Anneka was about to reveal something even weirder.

"And then, what, Mrs. Lund?" Sergeant Detree said, almost cooing.

"And then on my way off the property, I saw a couple sitting on a kayak totally naked, just a few yards off shore."

"Can you describe them in more detail?" Sabrina asked.

"They were fat."

Chapter Thirty-Two

Sabrina stayed to finish washing the dishes after Lucy Detree left. Anneka and Gavin departed a little later, leaving Sabrina alone with her thoughts. Henry was coming to Villa Nirvana shortly to help her change beds and run the vacuum. Gavin would be staying at the house after he returned Anneka to the Westin.

The monotony of washing dish after dish was comforting to Sabrina. Although there was a dishwasher, it would take so many loads to do all the plates, Sabrina would have to stay at Villa Nirvana for hours. There was something toxic about the villa, and Sabrina couldn't wait to leave.

"Inside."

Sabrina knew it was Henry calling out to let her know he had arrived. She went to greet him in the great room, ushering him into the kitchen where she handed him a dishtowel.

"Here, dry while I fill you in," she said.

She reported all the information she had compiled since the morning, starting with Heather denying the necklace was in her pocket.

"That's bizarre, especially since she knows you did the laundry," Henry said.

"But it's the skinny-dippers I need to tell you about. I think they may have killed Elena."

Sabrina described what she had learned from Lucy Detree about the floating red hibiscus.

"Definitely not Elena's," Henry agreed.

"But wait until you hear what Anneka had to say," Sabrina recounted Anneka's tale of cautioning Elena and then witnessing her signature on the prenup.

"The bombshell came when Anneka claimed to have seen two fat naked people sitting on a kayak by Ditleff Beach, just a short way off shore."

"Holy shit. But why would a couple of nutty skinny-dippers want to kill Elena?"

Sabrina's cell phone began playing "Locked Away."

"You need a new ring tone. That song is so uncool," Henry said. She knew he loved to tease her and, if she was honest, she enjoyed it, particularly at a moment like this when she needed to feel like there was some normalcy left in her life.

The sound of Neil's voice soothed her even more.

"Salty, we're back. Can you come and get us at the dock? We need to find somewhere we can talk and regroup. Somewhere private. And Sean needs to be there."

Sabrina was encouraged by the anticipation she could hear in Neil's voice. Where could they meet that was private? Not her place if that reporter was still stalking her. Certainly not Bar None. Henry's gated condominium community seemed like the best option. Besides, Girlfriend was there.

"How about Henry's?" Henry gave her a quizzical glance.

Sabrina got off the phone and explained that he should go and pick up Neil and David while she went to find Sean so they could meet at Henry's condo.

"Whatever Neil and David learned, they want to share where we'll have some privacy. You're the only one in our circle who's got that, my dear."

"But that means David gets to see where I live and the place is a sight," Henry moaned.

"Henry, your place is so neat, it makes me nervous. Besides, Ten Villas' reputation and real estate license are at stake. And don't forget, you were one of the last people to see Elena alive. It's more important for us to strategize than to worry about our love lives at the moment."

Sabrina reached Sean on his cell phone and offered to drive him to Henry's condo since he didn't know the way, but Sean said he'd find it and meet her there. She reached Henry's within ten minutes and was surprised when Sean pulled up right behind her at the latched gate. She hit the code on the number pad, pointing to Sean where he should park.

"I hope Neil learned something in San Juan," Sean said as Sabrina opened the door to the condo with her own key. She hoped so too, for everyone's sake, but particularly for Sean, whose face was beginning to look gaunt.

They were greeted at the door by Henry and Girlfriend, whose tail wagged at a rate close to a hummingbird's wings. Sabrina bent to let her beloved pet nuzzle her, enjoying the few seconds of uncomplicated comfort before hearing whatever news Neil had for them.

Henry gave Sean a handshake and ushered them into his sleek black-and-white living room. Neil rose from a white leather chair, while a tiny gray-haired woman remained seated on the edge of the oversized black leather couch. She was wearing a faded yellow sundress and had a white mohair throw wrapped around her shoulders, the same one Sabrina always tucked under because Henry kept the temperature so low.

"Where's David?" Sabrina whispered to Henry.

"He thought I might be uncomfortable having him in my home, so he took a cab back to Gibney," Henry said. Sabrina nodded, thinking "Operation Whatever It Takes" was off to a fine start.

"Sean, David and I were able to find more information for you after Sabrina told me about Elena's friend at the *caserio*. Some of it may be difficult for you to hear. Please let me introduce Elena's mother, Carmen Perez Pagan," Neil said.

Sean looked over at the small woman on the couch and then back to Neil.

"Pagan? I don't understand." Sean's expression was anguished. Had he reached his capacity for torment? She remembered a time in her life when she thought she could bear no more pain, but when it kept coming, somehow her capacity for it grew.

"Please, have a seat," Henry said, motioning Sean to the empty seat next to Mrs. Pagan, who remained at the edge of the couch, staring at Sean.

Sean sat down, nodding to Mrs. Pagan, who offered him the barest shadow of a smile.

"It would be better if Carmen told you the story." Neil returned to his chair. Sabrina and Henry sat on the empty love seat opposite the couch.

"I am sorry to meet you like this. I never thought it would turn out this way. I only wanted a better life for my daughter. And now she is dead after all. I think God must be punishing me for my lies." Carmen reached for a tissue from the box Henry slid in front of her on the glass coffee table.

"Tell me. Please," Sean said, grabbing a tissue of his own. Sabrina wondered if Sean had ever cried as a grown man before Elena's death. So many men suppressed their tears. So did some women. She was one of them.

"My daughter's name is, was, Angelica Pagan Perez. She was my only child. I had to have an emergency surgery when she was born and so there could be no others.

Her father left us to move to New York when Angelica was still a baby. We were very poor like everyone else who lived at the *caserio*," Carmen twisted the tissue in her hand.

"Angelica? Angel," Sean said, sinking back into the couch.

Henry slipped off the loveseat, stepping over to the coffee table, where Sabrina noticed for the first time that a chilled bottle of Chardonnay sat next to six wine glasses. He silently poured the wine into a glass, sliding one over to Carmen, then another over to Sean. Sabrina loved Henry for knowing exactly when and how to comfort people.

Carmen accepted the wine and took a small sip.

"*Gracias*," she said to Henry.

"I worked at a hotel cleaning rooms. Angelica was a good girl, never getting in trouble. She worked so hard in school because she said she hated living in the *caserio* where there were drugs and bad things always happening everywhere around us. Gangs would fight with each other. Everyone seemed to have a gun or a knife. It wasn't safe for a young girl to go anywhere alone, even in the daytime." Carmen's eyes gazed off into the distance, as if she were back in the *caserio*.

"Carmen still lives there, Sean. In the same apartment. It's still a rough neighborhood, although much of it has been torn down," Neil said, pouring a glass of wine and handing it to Sabrina. Sabrina's hands shook a little as she took a sip. She wondered what Sean must be feeling.

"Angelica was determined she would get good grades and apply for a scholarship to college, but we both knew there wasn't much chance of that. Our schools are so bad, even with good grades, it is hard to advance. Still, she kept working hard to get straight A's and tried some sports she thought might help with getting her into a college. But she was tiny, you know, like me, and sports weren't her strength." Carmen turned her body toward Sean.

"She couldn't even play miniature golf well," Sean said, chuckling softly and turning to face Carmen, who smiled back.

"Her best friend was a classmate who also lived in the *caserio*. Elena lived in a high-rise with her parents and brother and sisters. It was always noisy and crowded at Elena's home, so they would study here together. Besides, two of Elena's brothers were in gangs, and Elena didn't feel safe because the gangs were always fighting. Killing each other."

"I can't imagine," Sabrina said, transported mentally back to Allerton, a working-class seaside town south of Boston where she grew up feeling underprivileged at best. Maybe it hadn't been as bad as she thought.

"The day of the explosion, Elena was supposed to come to our apartment to work on a school project and sleep over. They were in the ninth grade and had to compile information about each of the American states. Elena was late, so Angelica began without her. I still remember she was explaining to me that Albany was the capital of New

York, not New York City as I thought. See, I was learning from my fourteen-year-old girl. That was when we felt the explosion. The whole building shook, even though it happened at the other end of the projects. We heard sirens and more explosions. There was smoke everywhere. We had to leave our own building. I thought we were at war. I guess we were," Carmen said, taking the last sip of the white wine.

"How did Angelica become Elena?" Sean asked. His eyes were brimming with tears. Sabrina was surprised to find hers were as well.

"Everyone was evacuated. They opened the schools for us to go to. The American Red Cross brought blankets and cots. We learned everyone in Elena's building had died." Carmen nodded when Henry offered to refill her glass.

"We checked the records, Sean. The entire building imploded after a cannonball of fire engulfed it. There were no survivors. It was impossible to identify the remains. They'd been incinerated, almost like they were cremated. There was total chaos. The only survivors were the few fortunate people who weren't home when the explosion occurred," Neil added.

"There were a number of adults who were working second shift, but most children were at home because it was after school. While Angelica and I were staying at a school, the Red Cross announced that there was a program for the children orphaned by the disaster. Younger children were being placed with extended family, if they had any, or with foster families. High school kids without surviving family were being offered placement at a Catholic residential academy in New Orleans." Carmen dabbed the corner of her eyes with a tissue.

"Angelica saw her opportunity to get out of the *caserio* and to get an education," Sabrina said without thinking. Now she got it. Sean's Elena was a daring, scrappy survivor—a fourteen-year-old girl who had grabbed a chance for a new life out of the embers of someone else's tragedy. Wouldn't she have done the same if she could have escaped Allerton?

"Yes. She begged me. 'Please, Mama, please.' It felt crazy to let my young daughter go out into the world alone like that, but I have to admit, I saw how it could work. I walked her to the church where they had instructed the high school students to go to be considered. I told her I would wait outside in case they said no or figured out she wasn't Elena. She laughed and told me they would never guess otherwise. I waited outside of that church until dark, hoping she would come back to me. It was the last time I ever saw her." Carmen wept, covering her face with her hands. Sean reached over and placed a hand on her shoulder, while the tears streamed down his own face.

"But surely, you heard from her, didn't you?" Henry asked. He couldn't comprehend families like Sabrina's and Elena's. He had grown up "normal."

"No, she never did. Carmen had agreed never to try to contact Angelica until after she was safely out of school and educated. Angelica promised to reach out when she finished school. Carmen kept her promise. Angelica didn't keep hers," Neil said.

"And you told people you had sent Angelica to live in New York with her father, where it was safe," Sean said softly.

"Yes. Everyone believed me. How did you know?"

"She told me her friend had saved her life, that she was her 'angel' and had moved to New York away from the *caserio*."

Henry left the room and returned with a new bottle of Chardonnay. He poured Carmen a full glass and then refilled the others'.

"Are you saying you never even got a Christmas card from Angelica?" Henry asked.

Carmen shook her head.

"How did you survive? Did you ever look for her?" Sabrina asked. This story was much too close to her own, only reversed. Her mother had abandoned her when Sabrina was only two, never returning to rescue her from her alcoholic father. Sabrina decided Angelica Pagan deserved a mother like hers and that she deserved a mother like Carmen Pagan.

"I prayed a lot. I decided to learn English so I could talk to Angelica when we were reunited. By learning English, I was able to get a better job, and I saved some money so

I could get to travel to my daughter when she contacted me." Carmen shivered, pulling the throw tighter around her shoulders.

"I am so sorry," Sean said.

"I got what I deserved. I lied and cheated and God is punishing me for that. He punished Angelica, too. She was a good girl. She stayed out of trouble. But later, when I kept hoping she would come back to me, I couldn't help but remember."

"Remember what?" Sabrina asked gently.

"She never once cried for Elena."

Chapter Thirty-Three

"How about I buy everyone dinner? You all must be famished after such a long day. I can get us a quiet table at Zeus, if you'd like." Neil stood up.

Sabrina knew he was uncomfortable with the level of emotion in the room, and she couldn't blame him. Unfortunately, she felt like she might add to it by bursting into tears herself any minute. Elena's story just hit too close to home for her. Sabrina made it a practice to shoo away thoughts of her own mother whenever one popped up in her mind, but Carmen Pagan's sacrifice for her daughter was a strong reminder that Sabrina hadn't been the kind of child who inspired such selfless devotion.

"Thanks, Neil, but I think I'm going take Carmen home to meet my family. I'd like to learn more about Angelica. I can understand why she tried to escape her childhood, but I don't get why we couldn't have finally included her mother in our lives. I tried so hard to get her to open up, but it was impossible," Sean said.

"And I want to learn about Elena, the woman Angelica grew to be. I need to hear as much as I can so maybe I can make sense of it in my mind and in my heart. I would love to meet the family Angelica had become a part of, Sean." Carmen took his hands in hers.

Sabrina gave her blessing for Carmen to stay at Bella Vista with the Keatings and offered anything she might need from the lost-and-found bags, but Neil had planned ahead and had her pack for a short stay. Within minutes, Sean and Carmen were off to Bella Vista. Sabrina thought about calling Kate to offer a "guess who's coming to dinner" warning, but decided she had done enough for the family. She needed time to herself to recuperate.

"How about you two? Can I buy you dinner?" Neil asked Sabrina and Henry.

"Thanks, but I'm going to pass. I think I need some quiet time alone, to be honest," Henry said, giving an uncharacteristically direct hint for Sabrina and Neil to leave.

Sabrina dragged herself up off the couch.

"I'll take a rain check. I'm too tired to eat," she said.

"I don't know what I was thinking. You know what you need, Salty? Water, not food. Salt water. You need your nightly swim with Girlfriend and then we'll check out your place and see if that reporter got tired of waiting for you to come back," Neil suggested.

"She probably did. INN has been all over a breaking story in Arkansas about a woman who fed her husband a casserole containing chopped up pieces of his dirty socks," Henry added.

"There you go, Salty. You've been trumped by a pair of dirty socks."

Sabrina chuckled. It felt wonderful to laugh after listening to Carmen's story and watching Sean's reaction to more revelations about Elena, who was becoming more mysterious, rather than less.

She handed the keys to the jeep to Neil.

"Here, you be the hero and drive," she said, letting Girlfriend into the backseat, making sure she had her spare tote bag with a swim suit and a couple of towels packed in the car. "Are you going to swim, too?"

"No, I'll pass." When Sabrina and Girlfriend went for their nightly swim, Neil would float in the water, sometimes falling asleep, to Sabrina's amazement.

"Good. You can be in charge of the diamond necklace," she told him. She pulled the baggie out of her pocket, where she had almost forgotten it had been sitting since Heather pulled her stunt that morning.

They glided down into the narrow streets of Cruz Bay as the sun began to set over St. Thomas in the distance. She still marveled that no sunset was ever the same and that she never grew indifferent to them.

Buoyed at the prospect of a swim, Sabrina explained why she still had the cursed necklace. She skipped the part about her conversation with Sean and his admission that he and Elena were apparently waiting until after the wedding to consummate their relationship, which Sabrina felt he'd disclosed unintentionally. It felt like a confidence she didn't need to reveal.

Instead, she babbled on about her meeting with Lucy Detree and how the skinny-dippers may have left their signature in the pool at Villa Nirvana the night Elena was murdered, making them possible suspects.

"Why would a couple of chubby skinny-dippers want to kill Elena?" Neil asked.

"Why would they want to go skinny-dipping in strangers' pools?" Sabrina countered.

She went on to tell Neil how Gavin had returned to Villa Nirvana and had tried to fire her and how Lucy Detree had actually defended her.

"That's encouraging," Neil said as they passed Mongoose Junction, lights beginning to twinkle from restaurants and shops against the fading light.

Sabrina finished the tale of her full day with the story about Anneka Lund acknowledging witnessing the prenup after Lucy Detree convinced her witnessing a document wasn't a crime.

"See, that's how someone like Hodge is counterproductive in an investigation. Why bully someone who's got information you need when you can get it by simply explaining you need their help and cooperation? Lee Janquar would never alienate a witness, and it looks like Lucy is taking a page from his manual."

"I just don't get the part about Elena saying the prenup was actually to her advantage when she had been wailing for hours because she said she didn't want to sign it. What exactly does it say?"

"I'll show it to you later and explain," Neil said. He pulled the jeep into the nearly empty parking lot at Hawksnest Beach, where Sabrina noticed two other jeeps were parked at opposite ends of the parking lot.

"Busy place," she said, letting Girlfriend out of the backseat while she grabbed her tote bag. She led the dog onto the path toward the pavilion, hearing Neil's footsteps behind her. Usually he would just hold a towel up as a screen so she could change, but if the interlopers from the parking lot were too close, Sabrina thought she might have to duck behind some trees to change into her suit.

She smelled the familiar scent of a mosquito coil burning before she saw the couple sitting at the same picnic table where she had shared lunch with Jack and Paul earlier in the afternoon. Something about the silhouettes of the couple prompted Sabrina to slow down and pause. There was just enough light left for her to see Paul Blanchard had returned to the picnic table. He was leaning in toward a woman and holding her hand on top of the table. She raised a glass and sipped what Sabrina guessed was wine.

Sabrina pivoted and placed her index finger over her lips, signaling for Neil to be silent, then pointed back to the car. Girlfriend retreated with her, resisting just a tad as Sabrina gently tugged at her leash.

"What was that all about?" Neil asked once inside the car with the doors shut and the engine running.

"I'm not sure, but that was Paul Blanchard having a rendezvous with Anneka Lund."

Chapter Thirty-Four

"Well there goes my swim," Sabrina said. "Maybe I should just find a pool at an unoccupied villa like the skinny-dippers."

"How about Maho?" Neil asked.

Sabrina agreed without hesitation. Although Maho Bay was at the far end of the North Shore beaches from Cruz Bay, it was conveniently located right next to the road. Their swim would be shorter, but she and Girlfriend would at least get one in.

"I was surprised to see Paul with Anneka. Holding hands. What's with that?" Sabrina asked, her head throbbing from all the twists and turns in the Keating saga.

"I have no idea. We've learned all sorts of information, but none of it seems very helpful in finding out who killed Elena. I keep remembering what the homicide cops in LA used to say. Look for the motive because the why leads to the who. But I'm still not sure why anyone would want to kill Elena."

"Tell me more about San Juan," Sabrina said, thinking of David as Neil drove past the gate to Gibney Beach.

"There's not much to tell. We didn't find anything more than you can learn on the Internet, until you called with the information about Angelica Pagan after some great detective work. Once you passed that along, we were able to locate Carmen after talking to a few people. Well, after David talked to them."

Neil slowed for the hairpin turn at the top of the hill before Peter Bay, much to Sabrina's relief. Sometimes he drove a little too fast for her liking even though she'd been a crazy Boston driver once upon a time. He pulled into a parking spot in front of Maho Bay, where there were no other cars or people.

"Hallelujah, Girlfriend, we are good to go." She slipped into her bathing suit behind a short seagrape shrub while Neil held Girlfriend. He finally released the panting dog from her leash and then took a seat at a picnic table. The sand still felt warm against her feet after a long day of full sunshine. The water was lukewarm and silky as she dove in and under to avoid the no-see-ums, which always seemed to prefer her to Neil. She felt Girlfriend splashing along next to her.

Sabrina began to swim toward Francis Bay, surprised to find herself crying as she pumped her arms and legs furiously, her chest heavy with grief. Salt from her tears stung her eyes, making her angry. The salt from the ocean had never hurt. Her ears pounded with the sound of her heart beat against the fury of splashes until she stopped, exhausted, and floated onto her back. Kicking her legs, she headed back to the beach, Girlfriend finally catching up to her as her speed slowed.

Sabrina emerged from the water, Girlfriend at her side, bending over at the waist. She placed her hands on her knees, trying to regulate her breathing and control her tears. She didn't want Neil to see her so out of control. So emotional.

Neil approached her with a towel, placing it over her shoulders. Sabrina remained crouched over. He rubbed her back.

"Salty? Are you okay?" he asked gently as Girlfriend began to pace.

Could she tell him, no, she was not okay? That having your mother abandon you when you're a toddler means you'll never be okay, even if you spend your entire life trying to learn to be normal? That seeing Carmen and the pain she suffered at the hands of a daughter who had callously deserted and betrayed her had triggered yet another painful realization? That the grandmother Sabrina had spent her entire life resenting probably had been so mortally wounded by her own daughter, she couldn't bear to get close to her granddaughter?

Neil reached for her arms and pulled her into a big hug, the kind that made her feel safe from the world.

"There's some good news. Your phone rang while you were in the water and when I saw it was Lucy Detree,

I answered. She said to tell you the skinny-dippers have turned themselves in and asked that you come to head-quarters tomorrow morning at ten," Neil said.

"Will Detective Hodge be there, Neil? I'm not anxious to be interviewed by him about the skinny-dippers or any-thing else without counsel," Sabrina said, recovering from her emotional tailspin and reverting to survival mode.

"Not to worry, Salty. I was saving the good news for later, but I guess I can share it now." He took her hand, leading her to the jeep. He reached into his backpack and pulled out a thick manila envelope. He started the car, turned on the heat, and pushed the overhead light on.

Sabrina thumbed through the raft of papers. A Petition for Admission, followed by an Affidavit in Support of Peti-tion with attachments including copies of Neil's bar card from California, his driver's license with a bad photo of him, and his passport with an even worse photo. The very last paper was Order Allowing Admission Pro Hac Vice.

"What do all these papers mean?" Sabrina asked Neil, who was wearing a mischievous grin.

"They mean you just got yourself a lawyer. I have been qualified to represent you and Henry and Ten Villas in the investigation of the murder of Elena Consuela Soto Rodriguez. Because Sean is the technical owner of the villa you manage, he gets to be included as a party I repre-sent," Neil said, beaming.

"How did you manage this?" Sabrina asked. "Does this have anything to do with the fact that you're reading a book about the Uniform Commercial Code?" She hadn't mentioned the book earlier because she didn't want to appear overly curious on her first visit to Neil's home.

"Um, no, that's something else. This is how a court authorizes a lawyer from a different jurisdiction to enter an appearance as counsel in a case pending in its jurisdiction. David made a stop in St. Thomas on the way back from Puerto Rico so I could get it at the court house. I should have told Henry and Sean about it, but that meeting with Carmen was so intense I forgot."

"So you'll come with me tomorrow?" Sabrina asked, suddenly overcome by a wave of exhaustion combined with relief and the need to get out of her wet bathing suit.

"It depends. Do you think you can you come up with the retainer, Salty?" He just loved teasing her.

"And what kind of retainer are you expecting, counselor?" Sabrina asked, playing along.

"How about a grilled cheese sandwich and a Guinness at your place?"

Chapter Thirty-Five

Henry wasn't as keen on solitude once he found himself alone. If he was honest, he had to admit he'd been disappointed when David had opted not to join everyone at his condo. Knowing David was likely at Gibney Beach Villas barely two miles away was making him restless. Having him on the same island was going to be nothing but temptation. What would Henry do if David decided to buy Larry's plane and cottage from Cassie? And why should he be the one feeling uncomfortable? David should be wearing the hair shirt, not him.

He headed to Bar None for a bite to eat, fighting the impulse to take a right turn toward Gibney when he reached Cruz Bay. He forced himself to turn left. Normally, Henry refused to pay for parking in Cruz Bay, preferring to spend twenty minutes driving in circles until a free space opened up. But tonight was different. He was spent. He plucked five bucks from his wallet without a second thought.

He found an empty stool at the bar and ordered a Bar None painkiller, which he hoped would perform. The bar was noisy and full, mostly with tanned young people talking over the noise and music. Henry's preference was to sit quietly and allow the din of the conversations to protect him from having to engage in them.

"Mind if I sit next to you?" a woman's voice said from behind.

He wanted to say, "Yes, you dimwit, I do. Besides, can't you tell, I'm gay." Then he realized it was Heather Malzone who had approached him. Henry knew he had caused Ten Villas enough damage in the last several days, so he decided to begin rehabilitating himself.

"Heather, please join me. I was just about to order some crabmeat wontons. What would you like to drink?"

"I'll have a double Patrón on the rocks with a slice of lime, please."

"That bad of a day?" Henry asked after placing the order. Maybe she was rattled by Sabrina showing her the necklace.

"I suppose you know—we now have Elena's mother with us up at Bella Vista?"

"If that's a problem, I'm sure I can find her a spot through Julie Lasota at Virgin Villas. Ten Villas is full until Thursday." Henry said, imagining how awkward life at Bella Vista might be.

"No, Paul is moving back to Villa Nirvana so Carmen can have his room. It's just gotten so very weird. To be honest, I wasn't wild about Elena, but I never would have imagined she was living a double life. Sean is so torn apart, I can't bear to watch it." Heather took a hit of her drink and sighed. "God, I needed that."

"Gavin's back at Villa Nirvana, too. Do you know if Lisa's returning?" Henry asked.

"I haven't talked to Lisa, other than when the cops were there, since I watched part of *Breakfast at Tiffany's* with her the night of the murder."

The new bartender Henry hadn't met yet slid the order of crabmeat wontons in front of them. They tucked into the appetizer without talking for a few minutes.

"These are incredible," Heather said, signaling for another round of drinks. Henry decided he would have one more, but that was his limit. Besides, it looked like Heather might be needing a ride back to Bella Vista, so he thought he'd better be able to drive.

"I can't imagine what it must have been like growing up with two brothers like Sean and Gavin," Henry said. "Were they like most brothers, teasing you?"

"Oh no. It wasn't like that at all. Gavin and Sean never did anything together. They were competitors. Gavin spent every other weekend with us making our lives hell. He would tell my mother and Jack these elaborate stories that had just enough truth in them that they would seem believable. They were always intended to get Sean and me in trouble. He would do mean stuff, like offer to take our new puppy for a walk, then let it off leash so it would get lost and we would go crazy trying to find it. Gavin hated it that he had to share Jack with us and was determined to torture us."

"Makes my life as an only child seem idyllic," Henry said, laughing.

"The weekends when Gavin stayed home with Anneka were like vacations to us."

"Did you have any clue Elena wasn't the person she pretended to be?" Henry asked, changing the subject.

"Not really. At this point, I'm not sure what I believed when—" Heather was starting to slur her words.

"It sounds like you know more than you're willing to say," Henry suggested, not sure if he should just come out and ask her about the necklace she'd denied having in her pocket.

"Sometimes telling the truth, Henry, can be worse than telling a lie."

"What do you mean?" Henry asked. He placed an order for a platter of Mix 'n Match Sliders and another drink for Heather. She didn't protest.

"Let's just say I'm happy Sean can have his memories, now that I don't have to dispel them."

"What about the necklace, Heather?"

"What necklace?" Heather asked, grabbing the last of the wontons.

Chapter Thirty-Six

Sabrina woke to find a cold nose nudging her cheek. Girlfriend had a sense of urgency, so Sabrina sprung out of bed, leaving a snoring Neil behind her. She poked her head out the door to make sure no one from INN had appeared during the night and let Girlfriend out on her own once she determined the coast was clear.

She put on a pot of coffee and grabbed the manila envelope Neil had left on the kitchen counter. She walked over to the corner of her living room where she kept her yoga mat and sat on the floor. Her legs reached up against the wall and she sidled her butt up next to it, her back resting on the yoga mat. Sabrina closed her eyes and took several deep breaths. Her morning routine was to try to meditate during this ritual, but this morning she didn't have time, so she was going to have to cheat and just read Neil's papers.

She read the Pro Hac Vice order again quickly, comforted by the news Neil could be her advocate. Next, she took the thick document that was titled, "Antenuptial

Agreement between Sean Michael Keating and Elena Consuela Soto Rodriguez." Sabrina wondered why everyone referred to the document as a prenup, when it was titled "antenuptial." She would put that on her list of questions for Neil.

The first ten pages seemed to be boilerplate, so Sabrina skipped to the end like she often did when she wasn't sure if she should continue reading a novel. Life was hard enough without unhappy endings, so even if it was considered cheating, she flipped to the end of a book if she was in doubt. The end of the document was simply pages and pages of financial disclosures. Sabrina noted that Sean's finances took up eleven pages, while Elena's only took up two. Sean's net worth was at least ten times more than Elena's. On the last page, there was a category called "Anticipated Asset Acquisition" in which Sean disclosed that upon his father's retirement in three years, 50 percent of the stock in Keating Construction would vest in Sean. Sabrina assumed the other 50 percent would vest in Gavin.

She leafed back to the middle to see what would happen if there were a death or divorce, which Sabrina knew was the whole point of a prenup. There was a general recitation noting that Elena was a valuable employee of Keating Construction as of the date the parties entered the agreement and married. If Sean died, Elena was protected by a large life insurance policy, which was to be paid and maintained by the corporation.

The provisions that would govern if there were a divorce seemed very straightforward to Sabrina. If there were a divorce prior to the third anniversary of the parties' marriage, Elena would maintain her position within the company at her current rate of compensation, unless it could be shown she should be discontinued for cause, in which case there was a mandatory arbitration clause if there was a dispute. Regardless, she would be precluded from claiming any right, title, or interest in Keating Construction or any assets owned by it.

If the marriage lasted three years and one day, Elena was entitled to the same conditions about retaining her employment and rate of compensation. However, she was also entitled to 10 percent of Sean's share of Keating Construction.

Sabrina wasn't a legal expert, but this seemed like a decent deal for Elena. Now she understood why the Keating clan had been perplexed when Elena had refused to sign. Her hysteria about the prenup seemed rather incongruous with her calculating, controlling nature.

The smell of the coffee lured her away from the wall and her yoga mat. She poured a mug of it and wrote a couple of questions for Neil on an index card. She could hear him in the shower and realized she needed to call Henry to let him know they had to meet at the police department at ten.

Neil appeared in the kitchen just as Sabrina was signing off with an uncharacteristically hungover Henry. In contrast, Neil's smoky blue eyes no longer seemed red with fatigue and his voice was chipper.

"Good morning, Salty. Are you ready for Matrimonial Law 101: Antenuptial Agreements?" he asked, accepting a mug of coffee from Sabrina.

She peppered him with her questions, getting the answers she'd guessed or expected. "Ante" and "pre" really meant the same in the law. It was like how a "separation" agreement was really a "divorce" contract. Sabrina got it. In her days as a meteorologist, she had used enough professional jargon to appreciate each field had its own language. Neil agreed with her that it was a pretty good deal for Elena.

"Especially the part about her only having to be married to Sean for three years before the property assignment kicks in. Usually you have to be married longer than that. The shortest I've ever seen is five."

Sabrina thought back to her spur-of-the-moment picnic lunch yesterday with Jack and Paul. It seemed like the whole Keating clan thought in terms of a three-year plan.

She went into the bedroom and threw on one of her generic "meet the clients" black dresses, which were now also becoming her "go to the police station" dresses. Sabrina pulled her massive curls back into a ponytail, regretting going to bed with wet hair once again. Showering after her swim and a grilled cheese had been her limit the night before, and she couldn't have been bothered to wait up while her hair dried.

"Come on, Attorney Perry. We're off to see the wizard. Henry is going to meet us there. He spent the night drinking at Bar None with Heather, who continued to deny knowing anything about the necklace."

Neil pulled the baggie containing the necklace out from the zippered side pocket of his khaki shorts.

"Well, you and I can do the same once we hand it over to Sergeant Detree, Salty."

Chapter Thirty-Seven

Henry was sitting on a bench in the lobby of police head-quarters when Sabrina and Neil arrived. He looked as disheveled as Sabrina had ever seen him, wearing a black T-shirt with navy blue shorts, a color combination even Sabrina knew didn't work.

"No matter what you're asked or told here," Neil leaned over and whispered to both of them, "Insist you're here only about the skinny-dippers. If someone tries to press you about the investigation about Elena's murder, tell them you'll be happy to come back, but all you're prepared to discuss is the skinny-dippers for now. Those were Sergeant Detree's instructions."

To the left of an empty desk, a door with a sign reading "Lobby Officer" opened abruptly. Two men in nearly identical blue pencil-striped suits emerged, followed by Gavin Keating in a crisp beige suit. Gavin looked over at them.

"The liquor supply needs to be replenished," he said. He filed out the door behind what Sabrina guessed were the lawyers he had special-ordered for the occasion.

Sabrina recognized Officer Milan, who came out of the same door and took his station at the lobby desk.

"We're here about the skinny-dippers," Neil said, stepping in front of the counter, which sat in front of Milan's desk.

"Are you sure about that? Aren't you supposed to be here about the murder investigation?" Officer Milan asked.

"No, not now. We're here about the skinny-dippers," Neil said.

"Well, it's just that I'm under orders to make sure . . ."

"Officer Milan, I assure you, we will return to discuss that matter later, but right now we are here about the skinny-dippers."

"Well, okay," Officer Milan said. "Come with me."

Sabrina, Henry, and Neil followed Officer Milan through a door to the right of the lobby desk, down a corridor Sabrina remembered from the last time she'd been interviewed during the Villa Mascarpone case. The air conditioning was on so high it felt like a meat locker.

Officer Milan opened the door to the same room where Sabrina had been interviewed before. She felt her stomach clench at the memory.

Inside at the long table, Sabrina was surprised to see Detective Leon Janquar, now known to her as Lee, seated with his left leg elevated on the chair next to him. Sergeant Lucy Detree sat to his right.

"Lee, what are you doing here? Aren't you supposed to be home, watching sports with that leg up on a La-Z-Boy?" Neil asked, extending his hand to shake it. Sergeant Detree stood and offered her hand to Neil.

"Murder knows no holiday," Janquar said, laughing. "But in this case, it's the crazy skinny-dippers who dragged me off of sick leave. Please sit down."

Neil put the manila envelope out on the table and began pulling out the Pro Hac Vice order. Sabrina was beginning to love those three Latin words, which for her translated to "I feel safe."

"I got an order allowing me to represent the folks at Ten Villas and the owner of Villa Nirvana in the investigation of the murder. I assume you'll honor it in this investigation," Neil started.

"Put those away, counsel. I don't need them. Why did you go to all that trouble?" Janquar asked. Sergeant Detree nudged his arm and wrote on the yellow legal pad in front of her. Sabrina, who had made it a practice to learn how to read upside down, read "V. H." Vernon Hodge, her favorite detective. Janquar rolled his eyes.

"Sergeant Detree tells me that the skinny-dippers have made appearances at three of your villas, Ms. Salter and Mr. Whitman." Sabrina wasn't sure when she had reverted back to "Ms. Salter" after being on a first-name basis with the detective following the Villa Mascarpone murder.

She hoped it was because he was talking to her in an official capacity.

They confirmed that Villas Mascarpone and Bella Vista had been targeted.

"We now know for sure, they were at Villa Nirvana the night of the murder," Sergeant Detree added.

"Yup. They came in last night, fortunately with their clothes on and with ID. I don't know what we would have done if we had to have a line-up," Janquar said. A ripple of laughter filled the room.

"What's their deal?" Neil asked.

"Publicity. Money. They're a middle-aged couple from Michigan, sick of snow. They said they watch *Vying for Villas* on some home improvement channel that runs a contest where you can win an extended timeshare in the Caribbean. They decided they would be more daring than the other entries they'd seen and would enter 'Skinny-Dipping through the Caribbean,' starting with St. John, as their bid."

"I've seen the show. That's a lot more creative than 'In Search of the Perfect Margarita,'" Henry said.

"Unfortunately, it's also illegal. When we let word out that we were looking to talk to them in conjunction with a murder investigation and would consider offering immunity from prosecution if they cooperated, they were here in a heartbeat," Janquar replied with a grin. "Of course, that means now that the skinny-dippers admit they were at Villa Nirvana the night Elena Rodriguez was killed, my investigation overlaps with Detective Hodge's."

Lucy Detree smiled at Sabrina in unmistakable glee.

"Well, I'm sure you will both work together to get the job done," Neil said, chortling.

"So what we have here is film from the waterproof GoPro cameras they both wore. They had them mounted on their foreheads. You're welcome to look at the footage from the other two villas later, but what I'd like you to check out now are some stills from the night they were at Villa Nirvana. They thought getting footage of the scenery where a big fancy wedding was about to take place would be quite a coup. I think they were considering selling it to someone like that unscrupulous talking head, Faith Chase, until we put out the word that they could be facing charges in connection with a murder."

Sabrina's heart skipped a beat, maybe two, at the thought of how close she may have been to another Faith Chase encounter.

Lucy Detree opened a file she had in front of her under her legal pad and pulled out an eight-by-twelve black-and-white photo that showed the pool area surrounded by the pots of gardenias, the tables and canopies above them lit with faerie lights. A second one showed the tabletops up close, with the miniature centerpieces of Villa Nirvana. The third photo was in color, the red hibiscus blossoms floating atop the surface of the pool.

The next shot wasn't as clear as the first three because of the lack of light, but Sabrina still recognized Anneka Lund sitting in an Adirondack chair on the bluff above Ditleff Beach next to Paul Blanchard, who had a bottle of champagne on the armrest of his chair. They each had a crystal champagne flute, which Sabrina noted was strictly against the villa rules she and Henry had promulgated not to take any glassware outdoors.

"Can you confirm who these people are? Sergeant Detree has done an initial identification," Janquar said. Sabrina knew he was letting them off the hook for implicating their guests by suggesting Detree already knew.

"That's Paul Blanchard and Anneka Lund." Sabrina was beginning to connect the dots.

"And how about the next photo?" Janquar asked as Detree slid a photo of Elena, alive and barefoot in her bridal gown, walking through the great room with a bottle of champagne in her hand. Around her neck lay the very necklace Sabrina had been lugging around for days. The one that now sat in Neil's pocket.

"You probably need to know about this." Neil interjected while putting the baggie on the table in front of Janquar. The detective picked up the baggie and held it at eye level. Without opening it, he pulled the chain within the baggie so the break was visible.

"Yes. I need to know all about this."

"Go ahead, Salty. Tell him everything," Neil urged her.

"When did you first see the necklace?" Janquar asked. He sounded a little stern to Sabrina.

"I found it in the pocket of Heather Malzone's dress when I did the family's laundry."

Sabrina started by explaining how she'd put it away for safekeeping and then forgotten to return it to Heather in the face of Sean's meltdown.

"Later when I picked Lisa up to collect her things from the Villa Nirvana, Lisa described a similar necklace she had found in Gavin's bag, which she was sure was a gift he was going to present to her for their anniversary. Lisa was trying to convince me Gavin wasn't such a bad husband when I'd mentioned bruises Henry had seen on her arms."

"Did you tell Lisa you had found the necklace?" Janquar was shaking his head.

"Of course not. Lisa has enough to handle being married to Gavin. I decided I would simply put the necklace back where I found it. I tried to give it back to Heather the next day, but she claimed it wasn't hers and handed it back to me," Sabrina explained.

"Did you know about this?" Janquar asked, turning to look at Detree. She shook her head and narrowed her eyes at Sabrina.

Sabrina could feel the interview going south.

"Hold on a minute," Neil said. "Sabrina entrusted it to me as her attorney. As soon as I determined I could serve in that official capacity—because Detective Hodge insisted I would be hung at sunset if I 'practiced law without a license'—we brought it here."

"All right. Everybody cool down. Obviously, I need to talk to Lisa Keating and Heather Malzone immediately. Can you arrange to have them brought in?" Janquar asked Detree, who nodded and left the room.

"Mr. Whitman, do you have anything to add?"

"Just that I was with Heather last night and she continued to deny having any knowledge about the necklace," Henry said.

"There's more you need to know, Lee," Neil interjected. Sabrina could have killed him for prolonging the meeting. She wanted to bolt, to be out of this room, out of the police station, preferably off island if the conversation was going to continue to suggest she had been withholding information or played any role in the Keating situation. It was irrational, she knew, but sitting in a courtroom day after day, hearing people testify that you were guilty of murdering your husband, tended to make you irrational when confined by the cops.

"Like what?" Janquar barked.

"Like who Elena Consuela Soto Rodriguez really was," Neil said. "I don't think Henry and Sabrina need to stay for that discussion, and I know they have things to tend to, so can we let them go while I explain what I learned in Puerto Rico?"

He had become her hero by taking the heat for her.

Sabrina and Henry nearly tripped over one another in their rush to leave the police station.

Chapter Thirty-Eight

Sabrina and Henry did what they did best in difficult times. They divided the labor and offered one another words of encouragement.

"It wasn't your job to investigate the necklace," Henry said when Sabrina expressed concern that she'd angered Lucy Detree. He was in charge of ordering liquor and having it delivered in order to restock the bar at Villa Nirvana. Henry would also check to be sure the rest of the staff had been attending to the needs of the guests staying in other villas. Sabrina, for one, would be so happy to return to their regular clientele. She wondered what the Keatings would decide to do with Villa Nirvana once the investigation was done. She hoped Henry would reconsider their management of it, but this wasn't the time for that discussion. For now, Sabrina would focus on putting the house back in order. Linens, floors, dishes. Easy tasks, compared to fixing human errors.

Sabrina drove out to Villa Nirvana, through the open, unattended gate, and out to the house. Two jeeps from

St. John Car Rental were parked by the front stairs, which she suspected were Gavin's and Paul's. Sabrina drove over to the parking spots by the service entrance near the kitchen to park. She noticed the trash bags she'd filled the day before and placed by the cabana shower stalls had been picked up. All that was left to do after the aborted wedding reception and the mess left by the police was to dissemble the chairs and tables. She would change the linens on the unmade beds and then leave the villa to Paul and Gavin.

She let herself into the kitchen, noticing there were new dirty plates in the sink. She didn't mind if they were Paul's, but couldn't help being irked if they were Gavin's. Sabrina placed the dishes in the dishwasher and went out to the great room to inspect what needed to be done.

She found Gavin sitting on a couch, his tie loosened, his shoes slipped off.

"Hello," she said, passing through toward the pool area.

"What are you doing here?" he asked, clearly startled by Sabrina's appearance.

"My job. I'm cleaning up the new dirty dishes in the sink. I'm having liquor delivered at your 'request.' I'm stripping the beds of the people who are no longer staying here and remaking them. Shall I do yours and Lisa's?" Sabrina asked, emphasizing Lisa's name.

"No, I'm moving up into the Master Suite. You can redo that one," Gavin said.

"Elena's room? You're moving into that?"

"I am, and I don't need any comments from someone who beat the system after killing her husband and can't even run a housekeeping business right," Gavin said.

Sabrina didn't even try to suppress her rage.

"Don't you dare talk to me like that. You are a rude, crude, narcissistic bore who just happened to be born into a life of privilege. You have a beautiful wife whom you abuse, three darling daughters you pay no attention to, and a loving, supportive extended family whom you have betrayed." Sabrina realized she was yelling but didn't care.

"You don't know what you're talking about. I am the glue that keeps this family business going. Do you think we would even be in this villa right now if it weren't for me and my vision for the company? Do you think my father or Paul would ever have dreamed of building anything other than parking garages? Do you think my half brother has enough brains to think like that? Instead of being grateful, they all complain. The only one who got it—"

"Was Elena," Sabrina said. She turned on her heels and walked up to the pool area and began dismantling the tables, which she stacked where they could be easily removed—on their sides, leaning against a stone pillar nearest the cabana at the edge of the pool. She collapsed the folding chairs, resting them against the tables. Then she rolled all the containers of gardenias, which were on wheels, into one area, next to the tables and chairs. She had created a minifortress of wedding props. It felt good to do physical work after her outburst. All the bits and pieces she'd learned about Elena's life and death, the dynamics of the Keating family, and even the politics of the police department churned in her head like a washing machine on the spin cycle.

"I'm sorry. He had no business talking to you like that." Paul Blanchard stood next to the pool dressed in slacks and a polo shirt.

"You heard?" Sabrina was more worried about what she had said that might be more insulting to Paul than anything Gavin had said to her.

"Jack and I won't always be around to make things right. I worry about what will happen to this family then," Paul said, but Sabrina didn't think he was really talking to her. She heard footsteps and hoped it was Henry bringing the booze. But no, it was Gavin in his swim trunks, arriving to enjoy the pool. He had a copy of *Men's Health* in one hand and eye goggles in the other.

"You can make up the room while I'm at the pool. Where are the towels?" Gavin asked.

Sabrina walked over to the cabana to the left of the pool and opened the door where a stack of fluffy blue-and-white-striped towels sat neatly folded on a shelf.

"Here," she said, walking away and letting him fetch his own towel. If she knew how, she would short-sheet his bed.

Chapter Thirty-Nine

"It's an amazing story, Lee, but I don't know that it has anything to do with who killed Elena," Neil said. He had shared all the information he'd learned from Carmen Perez Pagan and from the official records kept in San Juan.

Neil told Janquar where Carmen was staying in case he wanted to interview her himself.

"I probably will, but I think we'd better sort out this necklace thing first. Why would the bride be wearing a diamond necklace Lisa Keating expected to receive from her husband that then, according to your client, ends up in the pocket of Heather Malzone's dress? One can draw a number of conclusions. But instead of speculating, let me just talk to these women. Remember, I'm only talking to them because the necklace ended up on one of the skinny-dippers' photos. Otherwise, the issue would be investigated elsewhere," Janquar declared, nodding his head sideways several times in the direction of Detective Hodge's office.

Lucy Detree opened the door and leaned into the room.

"I've got Lisa Keating and Heather Malzone in the lobby. Heather arrived two seconds after Lisa, with her brother, Sean Keating, who says he insists on being present while Heather is interviewed. Lisa Keating says she's not talking unless she can come in with Heather and Sean."

"Sean's your client, right?" Janquar asked Neil, who nodded yes.

"Okay, he can come in, but if he gets mouthy, out he goes."

"Understood."

Neil stepped outside into the lobby to explain to Sean why he was at the police station and the parameters of Sean's presence during the interview.

"I'm cleared to officially represent you, Sean. I can't represent Heather, but if I think something is going wrong, I'll give you a signal so she can stop the interview and get her own lawyer," Neil instructed.

Inside the interview room, Neil and Sean sat to one side of the table, while Lisa and Heather sat in the middle.

"Where's that other detective?" Lisa asked.

"He's busy interviewing other people. Would you feel more comfortable waiting for him, Mrs. Keating?" Janquar asked.

"God, no. He makes me so nervous, I tried getting my husband to have the lawyers the company sent down come with me. But Gavin said that wouldn't be appropriate because I'm not part of the company." Lisa's jaw tightened.

"Folks, we have a photo I want to show you and then I'd like to ask a couple of questions. If you are uncomfortable at any time and want to engage an attorney, just tell me and I'll stop. Remember, the goal here is for us to find out who killed Elena, not to trick you," Janquar started.

Lucy Detree pulled the stack of photos out of the pile again, thumbing through them until she found one, which she placed on the table between Heather and Lisa.

"My god, that's my necklace Elena's wearing. How did she get it?" Lisa gasped.

"Do you recognize the necklace, Ms. Malzone?" Sergeant Detree asked.

"Actually, it's Dr. Malzone," Sean interjected, sitting back after getting one of Neil's "shut your mouth" glances.

Heather sat silently looking at the photo, and then over at Sean.

"Ms. Salter claims she found the necklace in your dress pocket when she was doing the laundry and that you denied it was yours," Detective Janquar said to Heather.

"You had my necklace? What's with that, Heather?" Lisa cried.

"It wasn't yours, Lisa." Heather's voice was barely audible.

"What do you mean it wasn't my necklace? I saw it in Gavin's bag." Lisa still wasn't getting what Neil knew might be too painful for her to admit.

"He gave it to her," Heather said. "To Elena."

"Why would he do that?" Sean asked. Neil knew Sean's IQ was fairly high. He marveled at how oblivious people in love can be.

Lisa sat very still for a few moments. Neil could see her fighting to control her emotions. Her lower lip trembled as she blinked back tears in her eyes.

"And how did you come into possession of it, Dr. Malzone?" Janquar asked gently. Neil knew Janquar expected he might be on the verge of a confession.

Neil looked over at Sean, who seemed oblivious to the implications of what both Lisa and Heather had said. Neil placed his foot on Sean's and pressed down gently.

"Heather, you might want an attorney before you answer that," Sean said.

"If you killed her, I'm glad," Lisa said. "You should have killed him too, the son of a bitch."

Before Heather could respond about whether she wanted to get an attorney before answering any further questions, there was a knock on the door.

Officer Milan opened the door and handed a few sheets of paper to Detective Janquar. "A fax just came in from the Medical Examiner's office, sir. Detective Hodge is at lunch, so I thought you might want to take a look."

Janquar scanned the pages up and down and then handed them to Sergeant Detree who did the same. The silence hung in the room like a thundercloud just waiting to burst.

"Dr. Malzone and Mrs. Keating, could I ask you to please step out into the lobby? Obviously, you can't leave, but if you want to make a call, Officer Milan can assist you," Detective Janquar offered.

Heather and Lisa followed Officer Milan out of the room. Detective Janquar signaled that Neil and Sean should move into their seats.

"I know you and Elena didn't actually marry, but you were very close to it, and I am sorry for your loss, Mr. Keating." Janquar looked directly at Sean and spoke in soft voice.

"Thank you," Sean said. He bowed his head. Neil thought Sean might cry again.

"We try very hard to be sensitive to the families of murder victims. We respect that you probably want to know what happened to your loved one, although how much detail a family member actually wants to hear varies. I've been handed the results of the autopsy on Elena. How much detail do you want me to share?" Detective Janquar asked.

"Think before you answer, Sean." Neil had seen too many clients say they wanted to know everything and then pass out when they heard about how deep a knife had penetrated their loved one's liver.

"Give it all to me. Please," Sean said. Neil wasn't surprised.

"Well, as you probably know, Elena was a very healthy young woman. She died of strangulation, which means she did not drown. She was dead when she entered the water.

We recovered her lace train or veil, which had caught on some coral. We think it was used to strangle her," Janquar said, taking a breath.

So far, not so awful, Neil thought.

"There's more, Mr. Keating. The medical examiner wasn't sure if Elena had been raped prior to her death or whether she might have engaged in some, shall we say, 'rough' intercourse before her strangulation . . ."

"What? No, no. NO," Sean's voice rose and he got up from his chair, running to the door and out of the room. By the time Neil got to the lobby, the front door was open and all he could see was the back side of Sean Keating racing down the sidewalk with Heather and Lisa staring after him.

Chapter Forty

Sabrina had put fresh linens on all the beds just to give herself the peace of mind that she was, in fact, a competent villa keeper, regardless of Gavin's unfounded barbs. Now she was in the lower level of Villa Nirvana, where there was absolute quiet as she washed, dried, and folded the sheets and towels she had removed from upstairs. If anyone had ever told her while she was a television meteorologist in Boston that she would find almost as much pleasure in placing order to linens as she had in forecasting blizzards and thunderstorms, she would have called them crazy. But with all that had happened in her life, Sabrina found soothing comfort in repetitive tasks, especially tactile ones. She could smell the fragrance of the lavender detergent. She could feel the softness of the sheets, the warmth of the towels as they came out of the dryer. She could lose herself in contemplation or be almost without thought. Today, she tried to muddle through the case, and its seemingly random collection of facts, to make some sense out of it all. But she was distracted.

Sabrina felt bad that she'd lost her cool with Gavin. Not reacting to someone like him was far better than giving him the satisfaction of knowing he had managed to reach her. "I will permit no man to narrow and degrade my soul by making me hate him," had always been one of her favorite Booker T. Washington quotes. Sabrina thought she had come very close to letting Gavin degrade her soul today.

The last load of linens was in the dryer. The liquor had been delivered and the bar restocked. She had only the dishwasher to empty and the three shower stalls in the cabana to rinse sand from and then Sabrina was done for the day. Maybe she would let Neil take her out to Zeus for dinner tonight. Or maybe she would cook for him on his boat.

She thought she heard the dryer buzz, and then realized it was her cell phone. It was Neil. Had he also been thinking of her?

"Hi there," she said, feeling warm and flirty.

"Salty, I'm just giving you a head's up. The shit has hit the fan."

"What do you mean?" Sabrina could hear the panic in Neil's voice.

"Well, Lisa knows Elena wore the necklace she thought Gavin was going to give to her. Heather's still not admitting she had the necklace. That was bad enough. Then the autopsy results come in and Sean goes ballistic when he hears Elena was either raped or had rough sex before she died," Neil said.

"Oh no," Sabrina said. "Where is he?"

"That's why I'm calling. He ran out of the police station and took off. I wondered if he came out there."

Sabrina explained that she was in the lower level of Villa Nirvana and didn't know if anyone else had come, but that Gavin and Paul were there.

"Neil, has Sean shared with you the nature of his physical relationship with Elena?" Sabrina knew she'd better clue Neil in, if he didn't know.

"Huh? No, why would he? What are you talking about, Salty? Do I know the details of their sex life?" She could hear the exasperation in his voice. He thought she was getting off track.

"Because there weren't any. They hadn't had sex. Elena was making them wait until after they were officially married," Sabrina said.

"So . . . oh damn, I get it. I'd better get Janquar and get out there. That's where he's likely to go, isn't he?" Neil asked.

"That would be my guess. I'll hold down the fort until you get here."

"No heroics, Salty. I can save you from the cops, but not from yourself."

Sabrina thought she heard him mumble, "Love you," as he hung up.

Chapter Forty-One

Sabrina clutched the pile of beach towels to her chest as she climbed the short exterior staircase to the ground level. She thought she heard shouting, so she decided to enter the cabana from the exterior of the house rather than around the pool from inside.

The cabana was a cleverly designed building almost the size of her cottage with an entrance from the parking area where beach goers could enter and use one of the three showers to rinse off sand. Pool goers had easy access from poolside. There were shelves with towels, pool toys, coolers, and snorkel gear. Beach chairs hung on hooks on the wall.

Sabrina climbed the three steps up to the cabana and opened the door. She heard loud voices coming from the area of the pool but couldn't hear what they were saying through the closed door on the poolside. She stepped into the cabana and placed the towels on a shelf. The yelling was getting louder but was still muffled. She cracked the door to the cabana and caught the words "killed" and "fool," but the others were garbled.

She remembered Neil cautioning her just minutes ago on the telephone. Bursting in on a family argument probably wasn't smart and was certainly beyond any role she had as villa manager. She was considering just hopping in her jeep when she heard what she thought was a gunshot.

The only other time Sabrina had ever heard a live gunshot not on television or at the movies was when she had fired the gun. In the dark. At her own husband. She felt paralyzed by fear and by the memory. Now she knew she really should run and get in her jeep and take off. Of course she should, but her keys were in her backpack in the first-floor kitchen instead of on her belt because she was wearing a damn dress today.

There was no lock to the cabana door from inside, so she couldn't secure herself and wait for Neil to come. Maybe it wasn't a gunshot. Maybe it had only been a car backfiring and her imagination was running away from her because she had also heard loud voices.

Sabrina opened the door to the cabana just enough to see Paul Blanchard standing at the edge of the pool holding a gun in his hand, pointing it at Sean Keating, who was crouched by the side of the pool. In one hand, Sean was clutching the hair of Gavin Keating, who was in the deep end of the pool. In the other hand, Sean held a string of the faerie lights Sabrina had just taken down, wrapped around Gavin's neck.

"Sean, let him go or I swear the next shot won't be in the air. It will be at you. For the love of God, don't be stupid," Paul screamed.

"I can't decide if he should drown or be strangled. You didn't give Elena that choice, did you, you son of a bitch," Sean said. He pushed Gavin's head down under the water, while he tugged on the cord at the same time.

Sabrina watched in horror. Sean sounded as crazy as she imagined he felt. His entire sense of reality had been shattered in just days. She wasn't surprised to find him over the edge.

"Let him up." She could see Paul's hand shaking as he held the gun in the air and fired into the sky.

Sean pulled Gavin's head out of the water. Gavin gasped for breath. His face was a very pale shade of blue.

"He raped and killed her," Sean raved. "He deserves to die." Sean pushed Gavin's head back under the water.

This time Paul shot the gun over Sean's head. Sabrina knew she had two critical situations going on. Paul could shoot again and hit either Sean or Gavin. Or Sean could kill Gavin, but then Paul could still shoot Sean.

She had to do something. Why were there always choices? Couldn't there ever be just one answer? If she tried to calm Paul down, would he shot her? Sabrina was terrified. She began reciting in her mind the mantra she'd used ever since she was a child, a gift from Ruth. *I, Sabrina, am not afraid. I, Sabrina, am fearless.*

Slowly she opened the door to the cabana and slipped down to the floor onto her belly. She kicked her flip flops off, knowing they were less reliable than her bare feet. She slithered on her belly over toward the stack of tables she had placed against the pillar that would shield her from Paul's sight.

"Sean, you've got it all wrong. Don't do this. Don't ruin everything for everyone over a woman. Especially this woman. Look at how she lied to you," Paul pleaded.

"He killed her, for God's sakes. After raping her. What do you expect me to do?" Sean said, this time pulling the cord but not dunking Gavin under water.

Sabrina could see better as she peeked from behind the table. She wondered if Gavin was beginning to lose consciousness. Paul must have wondered the same. He fired another shot, this one even closer to Sean's head.

Now it was clear. Paul had to be stopped or he was going to kill one or both of the Keating brothers. Sabrina didn't know if he was such a great shot, but between the shaking of his hand and his pacing by the pool, Paul was a liability.

She looked around her for something to throw at Paul, hoping to distract him and maybe get Sean's attention long enough that he would release Gavin, but there was nothing she could access from the floor. Neil should be arriving soon, but how many people would be dead or wounded by then? No, she had to do something now.

Then she saw them. She could actually smell them over the stink of the gunfire. The pots of gardenias sitting on circular, wheeled trays. Was she close enough to Paul? Sabrina tried thinking about how long a bowling alley was. The tile around the pool was definitely smooth enough to send the pot quickly.

"Let him go, Sean. You know killing your own brother will be the end for your father. If I have to shoot you to stop you, by God, I will," Paul said, aiming the gun toward Sean once again, his entire arm trembling.

Sabrina knew it was time. She popped up from behind the tables and moved two feet over to the flowerpots. With her best karate kick, she sent a pot over toward Paul, hitting him directly in the shins.

Paul toppled over forward onto the pot, dropping the gun, which skidded toward Sabrina, who scooped it up. She looked over at Sean, who was watching her and Paul. He let the cord go slack enough for Gavin to pull him into the pool.

Sean seemed shocked to be in the water, then headed toward Gavin, his arms flailing at him. Gavin lashed out at Sean with his right arm, but missed. Paul lay crumpled on the deck groaning.

"All right. Enough of this. I've got the gun now and I think you all remember I know how to use it. Right, Gavin? Remember, I'm the woman who beat the system?" Sabrina felt a little crazy holding a gun. Did she know really how to use it? Hadn't Nantucket just been an accident?

"He raped and killed Elena," Sean said, treading water.

"You stay away from him, Sean. Move away."

She had to keep them in the pool until help came. Otherwise, they could overpower her or worse, she would have to shoot them.

"He didn't rape her, Sean. How can you be so naïve? I think I've broken something," Paul said, sitting on the floor.

"We'll get you an ambulance soon, when help arrives, but why don't you tell us why you think Sean is being naïve, Paul?" Sabrina asked, buying time and keeping everyone in their place until Neil arrived with reinforcements.

"Because Gavin's greed and resentment had finally taken over any judgment he might have had. All those years I spent trying to protect him in the company, making sure he got a fair shake, and he was going to toss everything for a woman," Paul said, shaking his head.

"What are you talking about?" Sean asked, looking over at Gavin, who clung to the side of the pool but was not moving.

"Tell him about the three-year plan, Gavin," Sabrina said.

"Go to hell," Gavin spat back.

"How when your father and Paul retired in three years, you and Elena were going to take over the company, weren't you?" Sabrina felt like a prosecutor hurling leading questions at Gavin.

"He and Elena? What about me?" Sean asked.

"She was going to divorce you, Sean. After three years, she would have a tenth of your share of the company and with Gavin's half, they could pretty much do whatever they wanted. It was a very generous prenup, so much so that Elena was afraid you might renig on it at the last moment, which is why she led you to believe she might not sign. It was to be certain you didn't try to change the terms," Sabrina said calmly, not wanting to incite Sean.

"I don't believe you," Sean said, sounding deflated.

"She's telling the truth. I heard them myself that night. I went into the cabana to grab a cooler and heard them in one of the shower stalls, talking about Elena's great performance, how three years wasn't so long. How then they would own it all. I also heard, well, let's just say Elena wasn't raped, Sean." Paul's voice was grim.

"What about Lisa and the kids?" Sean asked.

"Gavin was going to divorce her, too." Sabrina said.

"So why did he kill Elena?" Sean asked. Sabrina could see his fury had been replaced by shock.

"He didn't," Sabrina said.

"I'm coming out of this pool," Gavin said, beginning to shiver.

"No, you are not," Sabrina said, pointing the gun directly at him.

"Please don't tell me it was my sister. Because of that necklace," Sean said.

"No, I think Heather probably ripped the necklace from Elena's neck because she knew it had come from Gavin. She wouldn't have wanted Lisa to see Elena wearing it. But Heather didn't kill Elena, Sean."

"I did." Paul began weeping. "In my entire life, I have never struck another human being, not even as a boy growing up, and then I end up doing something like this."

Sabrina was aware of movement over by the cabana, but she remained still as Paul continued. Both Gavin and Sean clung to opposite ends of the pool.

"How did it happen, Paul?" Sabrina asked.

"I was meeting Anneka after midnight. Oh, what you don't know, Gavin, would fill volumes. How I loved your mother even before she married Jack, and while she was married to Jack, but only after the divorce did she pay me any attention. I was the boring numbers guy. Jack was good looking and charming, but Anneka grew to appreciate my loyalty and devotion. She knew if our relationship ever became public, the family discord would only get worse, and she only wanted Gavin to have his rightful place in the family and in the business. So we kept our relationship under the radar for all these years, seeing each other only on the weekends when Gavin was with Jack while Gavin was a boy. Later, I was able to keep an eye on Gavin at work and guide him, as much as he could ever be guided."

"So, did you meet Anneka at midnight?" Sabrina asked.

"I was a little late because I got stuck in the cabana. I couldn't let Gavin and Elena know I was there and had to wait until they left. It was awful. I took one of the jeeps out to the main road, where I met Anneka and drove her back to the villa. We shared a bottle of champagne on those chairs overlooking the small beach. Anneka snuck into the house to see how it was set up for the wedding, even though I told her I thought it was a bad idea. But of course, that's never stopped her." Paul smiled briefly.

"Did you know she witnessed the prenup?" Sabrina asked. She could see Detective Janquar, Sergeant Detree and Neil standing inside the open cabana door.

"No, she kept that to herself. I was preoccupied with what I'd heard. I didn't know whether to tell Anneka what Gavin was plotting. And to be honest, I'm not sure she would have believed me. She loves that boy more than he deserves."

Sabrina glanced over at Gavin, who no longer looked defiant.

"After I took Anneka back to her car, I knew I couldn't sleep, so I took a walk on the beach. Elena was there in her bridal gown. Her performance was over and she seemed to be celebrating it with a bottle of champagne. I walked over to her and told her I knew about the plot she and Gavin had and that I intended to reveal it in the morning to Jack and Sean," Paul said, looking over at Gavin.

"What did Elena say?" Sabrina asked.

"She told me she knew I wouldn't do that because if I did, I would lose Anneka. I don't know how she knew about Anneka and me. Then she laughed, and I saw how truly evil she was and knew she was going to destroy the entire family. Sean. Anneka and me. Lisa and the kids. The business. And even Gavin. I couldn't let her do that. I grabbed the lace veil she had over her shoulders and wrapped it around her neck until Elena could do no more damage," Paul said, looking over at Sean and Gavin.

Detective Detree and four uniformed officers emerged from different directions, all with guns drawn, but Sabrina knew no one needed to use a gun anymore.

Sean swam over to the shallow end of the pool and walked up the stairs, his clothes dripping, his head hung.

Gavin waited for Sean to get out of the pool and followed suit.

Detective Janquar hobbled over on his cane, his hand holding a baggie for Sabrina to place the gun in. Neil stood behind him, waiting for Janquar to move out of his way. When the detective did, he drew Sabrina into his arms, holding her so hard it hurt. She clung to him, grateful for his strength.

Chapter Forty-Two

Sabrina could see Lisa Keating and Heather Malzone standing outside Villa Nirvana, watching the ambulance take Paul away. He was accompanied by a uniformed officer.

Sabrina approached them, wondering how much they knew or had observed. She led them into the great room, where Sean sat in his wet clothes, silently dripping onto a chair.

Sabrina was grateful that Gavin had gone to his room to put dry clothes on. She wasn't ready for another bout, and she was fairly sure that's what Lisa had in mind.

Heather walked over to Sean and stood before him. Sabrina hovered behind her, ready to help if needed.

"Paul killed Elena," he said flatly.

Heather remained silent.

Sean was obviously in shock, and Sabrina wondered if he should see a doctor. Gavin was probably in more need of medical assistance after being dunked under water so many times. They were both lucky Sean hadn't killed him. In some ways, they had Paul to thank for that.

Heather finally spoke.

"Someone has to talk to Mom and Dad, Sean. Do you want to come with me, or do you want me to do it alone?"

"I can't be there with her," he said.

"With Mom? I don't get it."

"No, with Carmen. I can't ever see her again without telling her how evil her daughter was. How she really deserved to die. How Carmen should never shed another tear over her. How she should be grateful, Elena—no, Angelica—had banished her from her life," Sean said.

Of course, Sabrina thought. Sean finally seemed to appreciate Elena's depravity, but it had taken epic events to get him there. She was impressed that Sean could still remain sensitive to how Elena's mother might regard his disdain for her daughter.

"I'll have them come here. We have decisions we need to make as a family," Heather said.

Leon Janquar, who had been lingering against a wall, moved closer to them. Even on a cane, Sabrina felt his commanding presence.

"Dr. Malzone, I agree. It would be a good idea for me to meet with them to clear up a few questions I have."

"Let me have Henry pick them up." Sabrina knew Jack and Kate would be devastated by the news that Paul had been the one to kill Elena and why. The least she could do was have someone spare them the white-knuckle drive.

The great room became silent when Gavin entered. Dressed in dry clothes, he had a suitcase in his hand.

"Now where do you think you're going?" Lisa asked. The outrage in her voice filled the room.

"I'm going to stay at my mother's. You'll have to move over here."

"You don't get to tell me what to do anymore, Gavin. I never should have let you to begin with."

As far as Sabrina knew, Lisa only knew about the necklace and had drawn inferences from it. Sabrina couldn't wait to see what Lisa had to say when she learned the rest of the story, especially about the three-year plan. Even with a prenup, Sabrina was pretty sure Gavin was screwed.

"Lisa, you know you are welcome to stay here or up at Bella Vista," Heather said.

"Yes. You're just another one of their victims. You and the kids," Sean added.

"Here you go, my man," Neil handed Sean a Bar None canvas bag emblazoned with the bar's logo: inverted martini glasses as the symbol of justice. Sean looked confused.

"Dry clothes, Sean. I am a full-service attorney." Sabrina saw a tiny smile in the corners of Sean's mouth. Neil knew how to do that. Sean headed to a bathroom with the canvas bag.

Leon Janquar whispered to Lucy Detree, who was standing next to him. Sabrina wondered what Detective Hodge would think when he learned Detective Janquar had broken the case. Oh, how she would love to be a fly on that wall.

Sergeant Detree walked over to Gavin, taking the suitcase from his hand.

"Please have a seat, sir," Sergeant Detree told Gavin, who didn't resist. He found a chair at the edge of the room near a window. Sabrina wondered if oxygen deprivation had tamed him.

"Has anyone called Anneka to tell her about Paul?" Sean asked.

"Why would we do that?" Heather had confusion written all over her face.

"That, my dear sister, is just one of the many secrets in our family that you are about to learn." Sean returned to the great room barefoot, wearing a Bar None T-shirt and a pair of gym shorts.

Henry arrived and escorted Jack and Kate into the great room. Sabrina's instructions for Henry, which had come straight from Leon Janquar, were that they only be told that Paul had been arrested for Elena's murder and that everyone was safe.

Kate rushed over to Sean. Jack followed right behind her.

"Are you okay? What in the name of God is going on here?" Kate asked.

"I can't believe Paul would ever kill anyone," Jack said.

At her suggestion, Detective Janquar told Sabrina that he would use the media room to conduct his interviews with the family. His first interview was with Gavin, much to everyone's relief.

Once Gavin was out of the room, everyone began to clamor for answers from Sean.

"Why would Paul kill Elena?" Kate asked.

"Why is he at the medical clinic?" Jack chimed in.

"How involved was Gavin with her?" Lisa demanded.

"I could answer your questions, but I'm not objective. I came close to killing Gavin less than an hour ago. I've had my head up my ass—sorry, Mom—for so long about Elena, it was like I was on drugs. You'd better ask Sabrina. She figured it out and probably saved all three of our lives, it had gone so crazy."

They all turned to Sabrina, waiting for her to give them the answers they needed. She could only give them the truth as she knew it to be, unembellished, without sparing feelings.

Sabrina started with Paul and Anneka's very sad love story because she thought it was the least painful and laid the foundation to understand why Paul did what he did. She went on to detail how Elena became involved with Gavin, their three-year plan, and their betrayal of Sean and Lisa, culminating with Paul's discovery of how they planned to essentially steal the family business and destroy the lives of all their family members in doing so, including Anneka.

Lisa had tears streaming down her face. Jack sat with his head bowed as if in prayer. Kate sat with her hand on Sean's shoulder. Heather rubbed her temples.

"I feel awful about Paul. We need to do whatever we can to help him. God, I may have killed Elena if I knew what she did," Jack said.

"I feel awful about Anneka. If I had any clue they cared about one another, I would have welcomed them into the family circle instead of being so threatened by her. I just couldn't let go of the past," Kate said.

"I feel terrible for my girls. What a sorry excuse for a man they have as a father. Sorry, Jack," Lisa uttered.

"No, we're all dancing around that issue, Lisa. I'm afraid Gavin is going to have to face the consequences for his heinous actions, the first of which is that he will never again be part of Keating Construction in any capacity whatsoever. Don't worry, dear, we'll take care of you and the girls, but Gavin is officially on his own."

Chapter Forty-Three

Sabrina met Henry for Sunday brunch at the Triple B, his treat. She ordered the Crabby Bene with blackened hollandaise sauce, her favorite. Henry had the Triple B Eggrolls, crispy dough filled with sausage, egg, and cheese. They sat sipping their hibiscus drinks—cranberry juice drizzled over prosecco—on a picnic table overlooking Coral Bay. It had been a week since Paul had been arrested. Life was beginning to feel normal again.

A cooling breeze whipped off of Coral Bay, making Sabrina feel more relaxed than she could remember. They had new guests arriving in the afternoon, so both she and Henry knew they had to grab the moment.

"If you give me your set of keys to Villa Nirvana, I'll drop it at the realtor's office this afternoon," Henry said.

"Sure." Sabrina took the keys off the ring she kept on her belt, which felt much lighter without the heft of Villa Nirvana on it.

"Sabrina, you do know how sorry I am about what happened at Villa Nirvana. When I think about you at the pool, with Paul shooting wildly with that gun and how you could have been hurt, I am overcome with guilt. I know it is all my fault. I should have listened to you to begin with. I hope you can forgive me."

Sabrina took a sip of her drink before answering. She was on the verge of tears. She didn't remember anyone in her whole life ever asking for her forgiveness.

"Of course I do, Henry. Don't be so hard on yourself. You thought Villa Nirvana would be a step up for us. I just disagreed. You couldn't know what a catastrophe the Keating wedding would be," Sabrina said.

"You are very generous with your forgiveness."

"Maybe you should be with yours."

"David? I know. Maybe I can forgive, but I'm not sure if I can trust again," Henry said. "He's buying Cassie's house and Larry's plane, so I guess I'll have a chance to find out."

"Think about how hard it will be for Sean Keating to ever trust again. Or Lisa," Sabrina mused aloud.

"Jack is putting the share of the business he was going to give to Gavin in a trust for the kids in Lisa's name. And he's hiring her so she can get some job skills. But no more vacation villas. It's back to parking garages for Keating Construction," Henry said.

"How's Carmen doing?" Sabrina asked.

"Julie says she's a great addition to Virgin Villas. Hardworking, pleasant. There's another person I can't imagine will ever be able to trust again."

"And yet people do, Henry. All in good time."

"What about you? Are you beginning to relax with Neil?" Henry asked.

"That is a work in progress," Sabrina said. "I may need a little time off in August when it's slow. Would you cover me? You know I'll do the same for you," Sabrina said.

"Sure. Are you going somewhere good?" Henry asked.

"I hope so. I'm going back to Boston to meet the grandmother I've never seen before it's too late."

Acknowledgments

Heartfelt thanks to my agent and friend, Paula Munier, whose editing skills are the perfect complement to her advocacy talents as an agent. Thank you, Gina Panettieri at Talcott Notch Literary Agency. Hats off to editor Matt Martz at Crooked Lane Books and his wonderful staff for their tireless support and nurturing.

I am grateful for the camaraderie of my fellow Sisters in Crime New England and the members of Mystery Writers of America/New England community. The generosity of the mystery writing community, most notably from Hallie Ephron and Hank Phillippi Ryan but also from too many others to mention, continues to amaze and impress me.

Editor Nancy Murray Young, we continue the journey together. Thank you for your generosity. For Julie Grant, my daughter who dares to be a first reader, thank you for your courage and honesty.

Thank you to the wonderful people of St. John in the US Virgin Islands, who patiently listen to and answer my endless questions and who endure my minor adjustments to their landscape and history. (There really was a seaplane service at one time!)

Steve Dorsey, you are my hero.

John Holmes and Victor Posada, I am so happy you are my family.

I am still saddened that there has been no justice or closure for the family of Jimmy Malfetti, who was murdered on St. John in 2014. Those who come forward are the real heroes in this world.

http://www.justiceforjimmymalfetti.com

http://www.facebook/justiceforjimmymalfetti.com